CW00941851

The Mountain Divide

by Frank H. Spearman

CHAPTER I

Night had fallen and a warm rain drifting down from the mountains hung in a mist over the railroad yards and obscured the lights of Medicine Bend. Two men dismounting from their drooping horses at the foot of Front Street threw the reins to a man in waiting and made their way on foot across the muddy square to the building which served the new railroad as a station and as division head-quarters. In Medicine Bend, the town, the railroad, everything was new; and the broad, low pine building which they entered had not yet been painted.

The public waiting-room was large, roughly framed, and lighted with hanging kerosene lamps. Within the room a door communicated with the agent's office, and this was divided by a wooden railing into a freight office and a ticket and telegraph office.

It could be seen, as the two men paused at the door of the inner room, that the first wore a military fatigue-cap, and his alert carriage as he threw open his cape-coat indicated the bearing of an American army officer. He was of medium height, and his features and eyes implied that the storms and winds of the plains and mountains were familiar friends. This was Park Stanley, charged at that time with the construction of the first transcontinental railroad.

The agent's office, which he and his companion now looked into, was half-filled with a crowd of frontiersmen, smoking, talking, disputing, asking questions, and crowding against the fence that railed off the private end of the room; while at the operator's table next to the platform window a tall, spindling boy was trying in the confusion behind him to get a message off the wire.

Stanley, eying the lad, noticed how thin his face was and what a bony frame spread out under the roundabout jacket that he appeared already to have outgrown. And he concluded this must be the new operator, Bucks, who for some days had been expected from the East.

The receiver clicked insistently and Bucks endeavored to follow the message, but the babel of talking made it almost impossible. Stanley heard the boy appeal more than once for less noise, but his appeals were unheeded. He saw symptoms of fire in the operator's eyes as the latter glared occasionally at the crowd behind him, but for what followed even Stanley was unprepared. Bucks threw down his pen and coming forward with angry impatience ordered the crowd out of the room.

He pushed the foremost of the intruders back from the rail and followed up his commands by opening the wicket gate and driving those ahead of him toward the door of the waiting-room. "Get out where you belong," he repeated, urging the crowd on. Stanley turned to the man at his side. "I will go upstairs to write my message. This must be the new boy, Bob," he added; "he acts as if he might make things go."

His companion, Bob Scott, smiled as he followed Stanley out upon the platform and up the narrow stairway leading to the division offices. But Bob Scott was conservative. He never spoke above an undertone and naturally took the conservative side: "If he only doesn't make them go too fast, Colonel," was his comment.

A tall young man, spare but almost gigantic in stature, standing back in one corner of the agent's office as the men about him were hustled along, likewise regarded Bucks with surprise as he saw him start single-handed to expel the intruders. This was the mountain telegraph lineman, Bill Dancing, as simple as he was strong, and ready at any time to be surprised, but not often disconcerted. In this instance, however, he was amazed, for almost before he realized it the energetic operator was hustling him out with the others.

When Bucks thought the room cleared he turned to go back to his table, but he saw that one man had been overlooked. This man was still sitting on a stool in the farthest corner of the dimly lighted room. The spindling operator without hesitation walked over to him and laid his hand on the man's shoulder. Dancing, looking back through the door, held his breath.

"Move out of here, please," said Bucks, "into the public waiting-room." The man rose with the utmost politeness. "Sorry to be in your way," he returned mildly, though there was a note not quite pleasant in his voice.

"Your place is outside," continued the operator. "I can't do anything with a mob in here all talking at once."

"I haven't done my talking yet," suggested the man, with a shade of significance. This, however, was lost on Bucks, who looked sharply at the stool from which the man had risen.

"I think this stool is mine," said he, picking it up and examining it. "It is mine," he added, after a moment's inspection. "Please move on."

"Perhaps before I go," returned the man with the same unpleasant irony, "you will tell me whether you have an express package here for Harvey Levake."

"Of course I will, Harvey," responded the operator in a matter-of-fact way. "Just wait a minute."

Levake's lips stretched into a ghost of a smile, and his white-lashed gray eyes contracted with an effort at amiability.

The operator, going inside the railing, ran over the express way-bills which, not yet entered up, lay on the freight desk.

"There is a package here for you," he announced a moment later, and turning to a heap of parcels thrown under the desk he searched among them until he found and produced the one he sought.

"Here it is—a box of cartridges."

"What are the charges?" asked the man.

"Four dollars and sixty cents."

The man laid down a twenty-dollar bank-bill. The operator hesitated: "I haven't the change."

Levake showed no sympathy: "That is not my fault," he returned.

The operator looked at him: "Do you want the package to-night?"

"If I didn't, do you suppose I would waste an hour here waiting for it?"

The boy considered a moment and made a decision, but it chanced to be the wrong decision. "Take the package along. Bring me the charges in the morning."

Levake made no response beyond a further glance at the boy somewhat contemptuous; but he said nothing and picking up his package walked out. No one opposed him. Indeed, had the operator been interested he would have noticed with what marked alacrity every man, as he passed through the waiting-room, got out of Levake's way. Dancing, standing at the door and with his hair on end, awaited the close of the incident. He now re-entered the inner office and shut the waiting-room door behind him with an audible bang. Bucks, who had returned to his table, looked around. "Well, who are you?" he demanded as he regarded Dancing. "And what are you doing here?"

"Who are you?" retorted Dancing bluntly. "And what are you doing here?"

"My name is Bucks and I am the new night operator."

"You look new. And you act all-fired new. My name is Bill Dancing and I am the telegraph lineman."

"Why, you are the man I am looking for."

"So I thought, when you pushed me out of here with the rest of your visitors."

"Why didn't you speak up, Bill?" demanded Bucks calmly.

A quizzical expression passed over Dancing's face. "I didn't want to break the calm. When I see a man walking around a powder magazine I hate to do anything that might set it off.

"So your name is Bucks," continued Dancing, as he walked through the wicket and threw his wet hat among the way-bills on the freight desk. "Well, Mr. Bucks, do you know what was most likely to happen to you any minute before you got through with that crowd, just now?"

"No, I don't know. Why?" asked Bucks, busy with his messages.

"Have you ever seen a shooting mix-up in Medicine Bend?" demanded Dancing in a tone of calculated indifference.

"No," answered Bucks in decided but off-hand manner, "I never saw a shooting mix-up anywhere."

"Never got shot up just for fun?" persisted Dancing. "Do you know," he continued without waiting for an answer, "who that polite man was, the last one you shouldered out of here?" Dancing pointed as he spoke to the corner from which Levake had risen, but the operator, straightening out the papers before him, did not look around.

"No, Bill, I don't know anybody here. You see I am a stranger."

5

"I see you are a stranger," echoed Dancing. "Let me tell you something, then, will you?"

"Tell it quick, Bill."

"There is no cemetery in this town."

"I have understood it is very healthy, Bill," returned the operator.

"Not for everybody." Bill Dancing paused to let the words sink in, as his big eyes fixed upon the young operator's eyes. "Not for everybody—sometimes not for strangers. Strangers have to get used to it. There is a river here," added the lineman sententiously. "It's pretty swift, too."

"What do you mean?"

"I mean you have got to be careful how you do things out in this country."

"But, Bill," persisted the lad, "if there is going to be any business done in this office we have got to have order, haven't we?" The lineman snorted and the operator saw that his appeal had fallen flat. "My batteries, Bill," he added, changing the subject, "are no good at all. I sent for you because I want you to go over them now, to-night, and start me right. What are you going to do?"

Dancing had begun to poke at the ashes in the stove. "Build a fire," he returned, looking about for material. He gathered up what waste paper was at hand, pushed it into the stove, and catching up the way-bills from the desk, threw them in on the paper and began to feel in his wet pockets for matches.

"Hold on," cried Bucks. "What do you mean? You must be crazy!" he exclaimed, running to the stove and pulling the way-bills out.

"Not half so crazy as you are," replied Dancing undisturbed. "I'm only trying to show you how crazy you are. Burning up way-bills isn't a circumstance to what you did just now. You are the looniest operator I ever saw." As he looked at Bucks he extended his finger impressively. "When you laid your hand on that man's shoulder to-night—the one sitting on your stool—I wouldn't have given ten cents for your life."

Bucks regarded him with astonishment. "Why so?"

"He's the meanest man between here and Fort Bridger," asserted Dancing. "He'd think no more of shooting you than I would of scratching a match." Bucks stared at the comparison. "He is the worst scoundrel in this country and partners with Seagrue and John Rebstock in everything that's going on, and even they are afraid of him."

Dancing stopped for breath. "Talk about my making a fire out of way-bills! When I saw you lay your hand on that man, I stopped breathing—can't breathe just right yet," he muttered, pulling at his shirt collar. "Do you know why you didn't get killed?"

"Why, no, Bill, not exactly," confessed Bucks in embarrassment.

"Because Levake was out of cartridges. I heard him tell Rebstock so when they walked past me."

"Thank you for posting me. How should I know he was Seagrue's partner, or who Rebstock is? Let's make a bargain. I will be more careful in clearing out the office, and you be more careful about building fires. There's wood in the baggage-room. I couldn't get out to get it for fear the crowd would steal the tickets."

"Well, you are 'out' four dollars and sixty cents charges on the cartridges," continued Dancing, "and you had better say nothing about it. If you ever ask Levake for the money he will kill you."

Bucks looked rebellious. "It's only right for him to pay the charges. I shall ask him for them the next time I see him. And what is more he will have to pay, I don't care whose partner he is."

Dancing now regarded the operator with unconcealed impatience. "I suppose there are more where you came from," he muttered. "They will need a lot of them here, if they carry on like that. How old are you?" he demanded of Bucks abruptly.

"Seventeen."

"How long have you been in this country?"

Bucks looked at the clock. "About five hours, Bill."

"Reckon time close, don't you?"

"Have to, Bill, in the railroad business."

Dancing reflected a moment. "Five hours," he repeated. "If you don't get killed within the next five you may live to be a useful citizen of Medicine Bend. Where are you from, and how did you happen to come away out here on the plains?"

"I am from Pittsburgh. I had to quit school and go to work."

"Where did you go to school?"

"Well, I didn't go——"

"Quit before you went, did you?"

"I mean, I was preparing for Van Dyne College. One of my brothers teaches there. I couldn't start there after I lost my father—he was killed in the Wilderness Campaign, Bill. But when I can earn money enough, I am going back to Van Dyne and take an engineering course."

"Got it all figured out, have you?"

"Then I heard they were building the Union Pacific, and I knew something about telegraphing—Jim Foster and I had a line from the house to the barn."

"Had a line from the house to the barn, eh?" chuckled Dancing.

"So I bought a railroad ticket to Des Moines from Pittsburgh and staged it to Omaha, and General Park gave me a job right away and sent me out on the first train to take this office, nights. I didn't even know where Medicine Bend was."

"Don't believe you know yet. Now that's right, I don't believe you know yet. You're a good boy, but you talk too much."

"How old are you, Bill?"

"I am twenty."

"Twenty!" echoed Bucks, as if that were not very much, either.

"Twenty!" repeated the lineman. "But," he added, drawing himself up in his tremendous stature, with dignity, "I have been on the plains driving wagons and building telegraph lines for seven years——"

"Seven years!" echoed Bucks, now genuinely admiring his companion.

"My father was a Forty-niner. I was a line foreman when I was seventeen, for Edward Creighton, and we put the first telegraph line through from the Missouri River to the Pacific," continued Dancing, ready to back his words with blows if necessary.

"You *are* an old-timer," cried Bucks enviously. "Any good rabbit-shooting around here, Bill?"

"Rabbit-shooting?" echoed Dancing in scorn. "The only rabbits they shoot around here, young fellow, are Pittsburgh rabbits, that don't keep their ears hid proper. When we go hunting, we go antelope-hunting, buffalo-hunting, grizzly-bear hunting, elk-hunting. Now I don't say I don't like you and I don't say you won't do. What I say is, you talk too much. I'll tell you what I've learned. I've learned not to say too much at a time. And when I say it, I don't say it very loud. And if you don't get killed, in advance, you will learn the same thing in the same way I learned it. Where are your blamed batteries?"

"Bill, you are all right."

"I am, am I?"

"First help me enter these way-bills and check up the express packages so I can deliver them to this mob."

"My business isn't checking up express; but I like you, young fellow, so, go ahead. Only you talk too much."

"Just a moment!"

At these words coming from the other end of the office, the lineman and the operator looked around. The military-looking man and his companion had entered the room unobserved and stood at the counter listening to the colloquy between the Eastern boy and the plainsman—for neither of the two were more than boys. Dancing saluted the new-comers. "It's Colonel Stanley and Bob Scott," he exclaimed.

Bucks walked forward. Stanley handed him a message. "You are the night operator? Here is a despatch for General Park. Get it out for me right away, will you?"

Dancing came forward to the railing. "How are you, Bill?" said Stanley, greeting the lineman as Bucks read the long message. "I am going up into the mountains next week, and I am just asking General Park for a cavalry detail."

"Going to need me, Colonel?"

"Better hold yourself ready. Can you read that, young man?" he asked, speaking to Bucks.

8

"Yes, sir."

"Lose no time in getting it off."

With the words he turned on his heel and leaving the office went upstairs to the despatcher's rooms. During the interval that the message was being sent, Dancing worked at the express matter. While the two were busy, Bob Scott, moving so quietly that he disturbed no one, laid carefully upon the smouldering paper in the stove such chips as he could pick from the wood-box, nursing and developing a little blaze until, without noise or fuss, he soon had a good fire going. In all of the mountain country there was but one kind of men who built fires in that way and these were Indians.

Such was Bob Scott, who, wet to the skin from his ride down the hills with Stanley, now stood slowly drying himself and watching Dancing and the new operator.

Scott was a half-blood Chippewa Indian, silent as a mountain night and as patient as time. He served Colonel Stanley as guide and scout wherever the railroad man rode upon his surveys or reconnoissances. Dancing, emerging presently from the batteries, greeted Scott again, this time boisterously. The Indian only smiled, but his face reflected the warmth of his friendship for the big lineman. And at this juncture Dancing, slapping him on the shoulder, turned to introduce him to Bucks. The three stood and talked a moment together, though, perhaps, without realizing what they were almost at once to go through together. The outgoing Eastern passenger train now pulled up to the platform and Bucks was kept busy for some time selling tickets.

His buyers were all sorts and conditions of men. And one forlorn-looking woman, with a babe in her arms and a little girl clinging to her skirt, asked the price of a ticket to Omaha. When told, she turned away to count her money. Among the men were traders and frontiersmen going to Missouri River markets with buffalo robes; trappers from the Big Horn country with furs; Mormon elders on their way from Utah to their Eastern settlements; soldiers on furlough and men from the railroad-construction camps on the front; adventurers, disgusted with the hardships of frontier life, and gamblers and desperadoes, restless and always moving.

Bucks needed his wits to watch the money that was pushed under his little wicket and to make change without mistake. There was elbowing and contention and bad language, but the troublesome crowd was finally disposed of, and when the last of the line had left the ticket window the waiting-room was pretty well cleared. There remained only a black-bearded man half-asleep in a chair by the stove, and in one corner on a bench the woman, who was trying to quiet the child she held in her lap.

CHAPTER II

As Bucks looked through his embrasure to see if all had been served, his eye fell on the group in the corner and he heard the woman suppressing the sobbing of her little girl. He walked out into the waiting-room to ask what the trouble was. He learned afterward that she was the wife of a gambler, but she told him only that she had followed her husband to Medicine Bend and was now trying to get back with her two children to her parents in Iowa. When she had ascertained the price of the railroad ticket she found that she lacked five dollars of the sum needed to make up the fare. Bucks had just a little money of his own, but he had counted on using that for his meals. While he was debating what to do, the elder child tugging still at the mother's dress asked for something to eat, and while the mother tried to quiet it Bucks felt he could manage somehow without the price of the ticket better than this woman could.

"Give me what money you have," he said. "I will get you a ticket."

"But isn't the train gone?"

"No."

The black-bearded man dozing near the stove had his ears open although his eyes were closed. He had heard fragments of the talk and saw the boy dig into his own pocket, as he would have expressed it, to start the woman home. After Bucks had given her the ticket and she was trying to thank him and to quiet again the tired child, the drowsy man rose, picked up the woman's hand-bag and told her gruffly he would put her on the train. As he started with her out into the drizzling rain, he carried her little girl, and, stopping down the platform at a sheltered lunch-counter, he bought a bag of doughnuts big enough to sink a ship. He offered no money to the man at the counter, but his credit seemed unquestioned. In the train the seats appeared all to be taken, but the drowsy man again showed his authority by rolling a tipsy fellow out of a seat and piling him up in a corner near the stove—which fortunately had no fire in it.

During all this time he had not said a word. But at the last, having placed the woman and the children in two seats and made them comfortable, he asked the mother one question—her husband's name. She told him, and, without any comment or good-bys, he left the car and started through the rain uptown.

After the train pulled out, the wind shifted and the rain changed into a snow which, driven from the mountains, thickened on the wet window in front of the operator's table. A message came for the night yardmaster, and the operator, seeing the head-light of the switch-engine which was working close by, put on his cap and stepped out to deliver the message. As he opened the waiting-room door, a man confronted him—the bearded man who had taken the woman and children to the train. Bucks saw under the visor of a cloth cap, a straight white nose, a dark eye piercingly keen, and a rather long, glossy, black beard. It was the passenger conductor, David Hawk. Without speaking, Hawk held out his hand with a five-dollar bank note in it.

"What is this?" asked Bucks.

"The money you gave the woman."

Bucks, taking the bill, regarded his visitor with surprise. "Where did you get this?"

"What's that to you?"

"But——"

10

"Don't ask questions," returned Hawk brusquely. "You've got your money, haven't you?"

"Yes, but——"

"That's enough." And with Bucks staring at him, Hawk, without a word or a smile, walked out of the station.

But Bill Dancing had seen the incident and was ready to answer Bucks's question as he turned with the money in his hand. "That is Dave Hawk," explained Dancing. "Dave hates a sneak. The way he got the money from the woman's husband was probably by telling him if he didn't pay for his wife's ticket and add enough to feed her and her babies to the river he would blow his head off. Dave doesn't explain things especially."

Bucks put the money in his pocket and started on with his message. The yards covered the wide flat along the river. Medicine Bend was then the western operating point for the railroad and the distributing point for all material used in the advancing construction through the mountains.

Not until he left the shelter of the station building did he realize the force of the storm that was now sweeping across the flat. The wind had swung into the northwest and blew almost a gale and the snow stung his face as he started across the dark yard. There were practically no lights at all beyond the platform except those in the roundhouse, too far away to be seen, but the operator saw the moving head-light of the switch-engine and hastened across the slippery tracks toward it. The crew were making up a material train to send west and the engine was snorting and puffing among long strings of flat cars loaded with rails, ties, stringers, and bridge timbers.

As Bucks neared the working engine it receded from him, and following it up he soon found his feet slipping in the wet mud and the wind at times taking his breath. Conscious of the folly of running farther, he halted for a moment and turning his back to the storm resolved to wait till the engine returned. He chose a spot under the lee of a box-car, and was soon rewarded by hearing a new movement from the working engine. By the increasing noise of the open cylinder cocks he concluded it was backing toward him. He stepped across the nearest track to reach a switch-stand, a car-length away, whence he thought he could signal the engine with his lantern. He had nearly reached the switch when his foot slipped from a rail into a frog that held him fast. Holding his lantern down, he saw how he was caught and tried to free his heel. It seemed as if it might easily be done, but the more he worked the faster caught he found himself. For a moment he still made sure he could loosen his foot. Even when he realized that this was not easy, he felt no alarm until he heard the switch-engine whistle. Through the driving snow he could see that it was coming toward him, pushing ahead of it a lead of flat cars.

Bucks was no stranger to railroad yards even then, and the realization of his peril flashed across his mind. He renewed his efforts to loosen his imprisoned heel. They were useless. He stood caught in the iron vice. A sweat of fear moistened his forehead. He hoped for an instant that the moving cars were not coming on his track; but almost at once he saw that they were being pushed toward the very switch he was trying to reach. Even where he stood, struggling, he was not six feet away from the switch-stand and safety. It seemed as if he could almost reach it, as he writhed and twisted in his agony of apprehension.

He swung his lantern frantically, hoping to catch the eye of one of the switching crew. But the only answer was the heavy pounding of the loaded cars over the rail joints as they were pushed down upon the helpless operator. Worst of all, while he was swinging his lantern high in the air, the wind sucked the flame up into the globe and it went out and left him helpless in the dark. Like the hare caught in the steel teeth of a trap, the boy stood in the storm facing impending death.

The bitterest feelings overwhelmed him. After coming hundreds of miles and plunging into his work with the most complacent self-confidence, he stood before the close of the first day about to be snuffed out of existence as if he were no more than the flame of his useless lantern. A cruel sense of pain oppressed his thoughts. Each second of recollection seemed to cover the ground of years. The dull, heavy jolting of the slow-coming cars shook the ground. He twisted and writhed this way and that and cried out, knowing there were none to hear him: the wind swept away his appeal upon its heedless wings; the nearest car was almost upon him. Then a strange feeling of calm came over him. He felt that death was knocking at his heart. Hope had gone, and his lips were only moving in prayer, when a light flashed out of the darkness at his very side and he felt himself seized as if by a giant and wrenched away from where he stood and through the air.

He heard a quick exclamation, saw a lighted lantern fall to the ground, felt a stinging pain in his right foot, and knew no more.

When he recovered consciousness, three lanterns shone in his eyes. He was lying in the mud near the switch with the engine crew standing over him. One of the men knelt at his side and he saw the thin, strong features of a face he had seen among the railroad men, but one that he knew then he was never to forget——the face of the yardmaster, Callahan. Callahan knelt in the storm with a good-natured expression. The men about the yardmaster were less kindly.

"Who are you, tar heels?" demanded the engineman angrily.

Resentment, which would have been quick in the operator a little earlier, had died in the few moments in which he had faced death. He answered only in the quietest way:

"I am the night operator."

"The deuce you are!" exclaimed the man bending over him.

"Who are you?" demanded the operator, in turn.

"I am Callahan, the night yardmaster."

"I have an order for you to send a car of spikes on No. , Callahan. I was trying to find you when I got caught in the frog." The pain in his foot overcame Bucks as he spoke. Another dread was in his mind and he framed a question to which he dreaded to hear the answer. "Is my foot gone?" he faltered.

The yardmaster hesitated a moment and turned to an older man at his side wearing a heavy cap. "How about it, doctor?" he asked.

Doctor Arnold, the railway surgeon, a kindly but stern man, answered briefly, "We won't take it off this time. But if he is that careless again we will take his head off."

"How old are you, boy?" demanded Callahan.

"Seventeen."

"Well, your foot isn't hurt," he continued gruffly. "But it's only God's mercy that I got here in time to pull you out of the frog."

The operator was already up. "I hope I shan't forget it," he said, putting out his hand. "Will you remember the spikes?"

"I will," responded Callahan grimly. "And I guess——"

"Say it," said the operator gamely, as the yardmaster hesitated.

"I guess you will."

CHAPTER III

Bucks, after his eventful first night on duty, slept so heavily that on the following afternoon he had only time to eat his supper, walk haltingly up the main street of Medicine Bend and back to the square, when it was time to relieve the day man at the station.

But the few minutes in the narrow business street filled him with interest and at times with astonishment. Medicine Bend, still very young, was a mushroom railroad town of frame store buildings hastily thrown together, and houses, shanties, and tents. It was already the largest and most important town between the mountains and the Missouri River. The Union Pacific Railroad, now a double-tracked, transcontinental highway, laid with ninety and one hundred pound steel rails, and ballasted with disintegrated granite, a model of railroad construction, equipment, and maintenance, was, after the close of the Civil War, being pushed with light iron rails and heavy gradients across what was then known to geographers as the Great American Desert, and the project of a transcontinental railroad was meant at that time to unite the chief port of the Pacific coast, San Francisco, with the leading cities of the Atlantic seaboard.

A railroad in building across a country considers first the two uttermost cities (its principal terminals), or those two portions of the country which it seeks to connect for the interchange of traffic.

The Union Pacific and its companion road, the Central Pacific, afforded, too, the first and last instance of the United States Government's becoming responsible for the building of a railroad. Although the project of aiding a railroad to be built somewhere between and connecting the Atlantic and Pacific Ocean ports had been discussed by Congress for thirty years before the fall of Fort Sumter, the extraordinary feeling caused by the Civil War alone made

13

possible so unusual an undertaking. President Lincoln himself had given the subject careful thought, and when, after much controversy and discouraging political intrigue, the Union and Central Pacific Railroad bills were ready to pass Congress, Abraham Lincoln was appealed to to decide a long-standing controversy concerning the gauge, or width of track, for the new lines.

After painstaking consideration, he decided on a gauge of five feet, but the promoters of the line then persuaded Congress to reduce the figures to four feet eight and one-half inches, and that gauge is now the standard gauge for all American railroads. It would have been better if the railroad builders had followed Lincoln's suggestion, since the traffic of American railroads has outgrown the possibilities of their gauges. And within a few years one of the greatest of present-day railroad builders has declared with emphasis that a six-foot gauge must one day come to provide our railroads with the necessary facilities for handling the enormous and constantly expanding volume of American railroad traffic.

The young operator, who, in spite of his efforts to conceal his hurt, now limped a little as he walked up the street of the new railroad town might well look with curiosity and amazement on what he saw. The street he walked in was no more than a long assemblage of saloons, restaurants, boarding-houses, gambling-houses, dance-halls and shops. Nearer the station and fronting on the open square, there were barber-shops and so-called hotels. Up and down the side streets he saw livery-stables and roughly built warehouses for contractors' supplies, army supplies, and stage-line depots.

The main street was alive with strange-looking frontiersmen, trappers, hunters, scouts, soldiers, settlers, railroad laborers, outlaws, prospectors, and miners. Every face that Bucks looked into presented a study. They were sometimes faces bronzed with the clear, dry sunshine of the plains and mountains, rugged with adventure and keen with dangers met and passed, but others were furrowed with dissipation and seamed with vice, or merely vacant with the curiosity of the wanderer.

Nearly every man carried a fire-arm of some sort. Indians were a continual menace upon the frontier to the north and west and on the front where the road was being built; and in the train-service and construction work railroad men usually went armed. Moreover, when the frontiersmen were not arming against the Indians they were arming against one another; it being difficult at times to tell whether the white men or the savages were the more dangerous to the peaceful pursuit of happiness. As Bucks, returning down Front Street, neared the square that opened before the station a group of army officers were walking across it. They were the first regular officers he had ever seen and he regarded them with interest. At the station the chief despatcher, Baxter, met him at the door. "Bucks, I've been waiting for you. Can you ride a horse?"

Bucks smiled.

"Colonel Stanley," continued Baxter, "is going to the front to-night. He wants to take an operator with him. Giddings isn't well enough to go, but he can take your key to-night; you can go with the colonel instead. He will take Dancing and a detail of cavalrymen with Leon Sublette and Bob Scott for guides."

The suddenness of the call was not unpleasant. It was such continual excitement and new adventure that Bucks liked and he said he was ready. The despatcher told him to hunt up Bill Dancing, who would give him the details.

Within an hour the cavalry horses were being loaded into a box-car up at the stock chute, and while Bucks and big Bill Dancing watched them an engine and the chief engineer's car were backed down the yard to make up the special train. At the same moment, the two saw Stanley walking across the yard with two engineers who were going to the front with him.

Bucks looked with admiration at the soldier-constructionist. He was slight in figure, wore the precise-looking military cap, and was dressed with extreme care. He stepped with a light briskness that implied an abundance of native energy, and his manner as he greeted the two railroad men was intimate and gracious, putting them at once at their ease. His smooth-shaven face, bronzed with service, and his brown eyes, were alive every moment. Whatever the enterprise, Stanley could call forth the loyalty and the best in those under him, and in Dancing and Scott he had two men that worked well together and had in their chief the unquestioning faith that insures devotion.

To these two more experienced men was now to be added a third, Bucks. The train started almost at once, and Oliver, the colonel's cook, prepared supper in his box-like kitchen and chopped his potatoes, for frying, in muffled ragtime, as the puffing engine slowly drew the train up the long gorge into the mountains. Bucks sat down at table with the engineers and Stanley asked him many questions. He wanted to know where Bucks had gone to school, why he had quitted at fifteen, and what had brought him away out on the Desert to begin railroading.

When it appeared that Stanley as well as he himself was from Pittsburgh, and even that Bucks had been named after the distinguished officer—John Stanley Bucks—Bucks was happier than at any time since he had left home.

The talk went on till very late. Stanley and General Park, who also had been a regular-army man, told stories of the Civil War, just then ended, and the giant lineman, Dancing, entertained the company with stories of adventure incurred in the mountains and on the plains in building the first transcontinental telegraph line.

Bucks sat for hours in silence while the three men talked; but he had good ears and was a close listener. All the adventure books of his boyhood reading had been bound up with this very country and with these rugged mountains through which they were riding. The tales of the people all about him during his youth had been of the far and mysterious West—of the overland trail and the gold seekers, of Pike's Peak and California, of buffaloes and trappers and Indians, and of the Mormons and the Great Salt Lake. These had been his day-dreams, and at last he was breathing the very air of them and listening to men who had actually lived them.

The sleeping-bunks in the car could hardly be called berths, but they served to lessen the fatigues of the night, and when Bucks woke in the morning he saw from his window a vast stretch of rough, desert country bordered by distant mountain peaks, some black, some brown, some snow-capped in the morning sun. The train stopped in a construction camp, near the end of the rails, and after a hasty breakfast Bucks walked with the engineers up the track to the headquarters of the rail-laying gang.

The air was frosty. During the night snow had fallen, and as Bucks followed his party the sun burst over the plain that they had crossed in the night and lighted the busy camp with a flood of gold. It was a camp such as few American boys had ever seen and of a type that no boy will ever see again. Everywhere along the cuts and hillsides and in sheltered spots the men had made temporary quarters by burrowing into the clay or soft rock and making dugouts and canvas-roofed huts, with earthen sides for walls.

But not all were so enterprising as this. Some laborers were camping in old hogsheads. Even packing-boxes served others for shelter, but were all so disposed within the cuts and among the ridges of the railroad grade as to be safe from Indian forays. And along the completed railroad, all the way from the Missouri River, material and supply trains were moving to supply this noisy, helter-skelter camp, which seemed to Bucks all confusion, yet was in reality all energy.

General Jack Casement, in charge, came forward to greet Stanley.

"And they tell me, general," said Stanley, "you are laying a mile a day."

"If you would give us the ties, colonel," returned Casement, short-bearded and energetic, "we should be laying two miles a day."

"I have turned the Missouri River country upside down for timber," returned Stanley. "The trouble is to get the material forward over a single track so many hundred miles. However, we shall be getting ties down the Spider Water within two weeks. I am on my way up there now to see what the contractors are doing."

It was the first intimation Bucks had had as to the object of the trip. Casement had a number of subjects to lay before his superior while within consulting distance, and Bob Scott, an hour later, announced that Stanley would not move on for two days. This left his attendants free, and when Scott, low-voiced and good-natured, asked Bucks if he wanted to go out on the Sweet Grass Plains with him after an antelope, Bucks accepted eagerly. The two saddled horses and Bucks, with a rifle borrowed from Sublette, followed Scott across a low-lying range of hills broken by huge stone crags and studded with wind-blown and stunted cedars, out upon the far-reaching expanse of an open plain. The scene was inspiring, but impressions crowded so fast one upon another that the boy from the Alleghanies could realize only that he was filled with sensations of delight as his wiry buckskin clattered furiously along the faint trail that carried him and his guide to the north and west. The sun was high when Scott reined up and, dismounting, tethered his horse in a glade hidden by a grove of aspens and bade Bucks do the same.

"Getting hungry?" asked Scott, smiling at his companion. An answer was written pretty plainly on Bucks's face.

"Didn't bring anything to eat, did you?" suggested Scott.

Bucks looked blank. "I never thought of it," he exclaimed. "Did you bring anything?"

"Nothing but this," answered Scott, holding up a small buckskin sack fitted with drawing strings.

"What is that, Bob?"

"It is what I carry wherever I ride. I carry nothing else. And it is only a little bag of salt."

"A bag of salt!" cried Bucks. "Do you eat salt?"

"Wait and see," answered the scout. "Pull your belt up a notch. We've got a little walking to do."

Scott, though of Chippewa blood, had been captured when a boy by the Sioux and, adopted into the tribe, had lived with them for years. He knew the mountains better than any man that served Stanley, and the latter trusted him implicitly—nor was the confidence ever betrayed.

Walking rapidly over a low-lying divide beyond which lay a broad valley marking the course of a shallow creek, Scott paused behind a clump of cedars to scan the country. He expected to find antelope along the creek, but could see none in any direction. Half a mile more of scouting explained the absence of game, and Scott pointed out to Bucks the trail of an Indian hunting party that had passed up the valley in the morning. They were Cheyennes, Scott told his companion, three warriors and two squaws—reading the information from signs that were as plain to him as print—though Bucks understood nothing of it. In the circumstances there was nothing for it but a fresh venture, and, remounting, the Indian led the boy ten miles farther north to where the plains stretched in a succession of magnificent plateaus, toward the Sleepy Cat Mountains.

"We are in real Sioux country now," observed Scott, as he again dismounted. "And we are as likely now to uncover a war party as a herd of antelope."

"What should you do, Bob, if we met Sioux?"

"Run," smiled Bob, with Indian terseness. Yet somehow the boy felt that Bob, in spite of what he said, would not run, and he realized for a moment the apprehension of one but newly arrived on the frontier, and still subject to tremors for his scalp. The scout took his stand near a thicket of quaking asp and almost at once sighted a band of antelope. Taking Bucks, he worked around the wind toward the band, and directed him how and when to shoot if he got a chance. Bucks, highly wrought up after the long crawl to get within range, did get a chance, and with his heart beating like a trip-hammer, covered a buck and fired. The scout shot immediately afterward, and the herd broke swiftly for the timber along the creek. But Bucks, as well as his experienced companion, had brought down an antelope.

Scott, as he joined his companion, looked at him with curiosity. "Where did you learn to shoot?"

17

"I couldn't do it again, Bob," exclaimed Bucks frankly. "The only shooting I've ever done is rabbit-shooting, or squirrel-shooting. I was lucky for once, that's all."

"I hope your luck stays with us. If it does we may get back with all of our hair," returned Scott. "The thing to do now is to lose no time in leaving here. We are farther from camp than we ought to be. When I get to running antelope I am apt to go as far as they do."

The two hunters got the carcasses across their horses, and acting on Scott's admonition started to cover a good bit of the distance toward camp before stopping.

The sun was already low in the west and Bucks realized that they had been out all day. The hunters rode due southeast, to put every mile possible between them and the Indian country before dark. They were riding along in this manner at dusk, when Scott, leading, pointed to a canyon that offered a hiding-place for the night, and directed his horse into it. Scarcely had the two passed within the canyon walls when Scott halted and, with a quick, low command to the boy, sprang from his horse. Bucks lost no time in following suit: they had ridden almost into an Indian camp, and when Bucks's feet touched the ground Scott was covering with his rifle a Sioux brave who with two squaws rose out of the darkness before him. Quick words passed between Scott and the Indian in the Sioux tongue. Bucks's hair rose on end until the confab quieted, and the scout's rifle came down. In an instant it was all over, but in that instant the Easterner had lived years.

"It is all right," said Bob, turning to reassure his charge. "He is a young chief––Iron Hand. I know his father. These three are alone. Eight of them went out after buffalo five days ago. The second day they fell in with Turkey Leg and a Cheyenne war party. Two of Iron Hand's warriors were killed. The rest got separated and these three lost their horses. Iron Hand," Scott nodded toward the silent Indian, "was hit in the arm, and with his squaw and her sister has been trying to get north, hiding by day and travelling by night. He can't shoot his rifle; he thinks his arm is broken; and the squaws haven't been able to kill anything. They are hungry, I guess."

"And did they tell you all this in those few words?" demanded Bucks incredulously.

"It doesn't take many words to tell stories in this country. If a man talked much he would be dead and buried before he got through."

"Bob, if they are hungry, give them some antelope."

Scott, who had meant to suggest the same thing, was pleased that the offer should come from his companion, and so told the wounded Indian. The latter drew himself up with dignity and spoke a few rapid words. "He says he is glad," translated Bob, "that your heart is big. And that it will be safer to go farther into the canyon. The Cheyennes are hunting for them all around here, and if you are not afraid to camp with the Sioux, we will stay with them here to-night. While the Cheyennes are hunting them, they might find us. It will be about the safest thing we can do."

"You know best," said his companion. "Can you trust this man?"

"Trust him?" echoed Bob mildly. "I wish I could trust the word of a white man half as far as I can that of a Sioux. He understands everything you say."

"Can he talk English?" asked Bucks in surprise.

"Better than I can."

It was with queer sensations that Bucks found himself in a hostile country and with the deadliest enemies of the white man going into camp for the night. Within a minute or two after Scott and the wounded brave had picked a defended camp near a rivulet of water, the two squaws had a fire going, and they set to work at once dressing an antelope.

Savory morsels were cut from choice spots on the carcasses and these were broiled by impaling them on long sticks over the fire. Bucks, learning very fast with his eyes, saw how surprisingly small an affair an Indian camp-fire is, and how much could be done with a few buffalo chips, if one understood how to keep them renewed. Both safety and convenience were served by the tiny blaze, and meat never tasted as good to Bucks as it did on that clear, frosty night, broiled by the two women and garnished from Bob Scott's provident salt bag.

After satisfying his ravenous hunger, which the Indians considered not even a fair appetite, Bucks asked to look at the warrior's injured arm, explaining that his father had been an army surgeon in the great white man's war, as Bob Scott designated the Civil War in translating for the Sioux. The arm, which was badly swollen, he found had indeed been broken by a bullet near the wrist, but only one bone was fractured, and, finding no trace of the bullet, the confident young surgeon offered to set the fracture.

Iron Hand, nothing loath, accepted the offer, and after cleansing the wound as well as it could be cleansed in running water hard by, Bucks took the rough splints handily supplied by Scott's hunting-knife, and pulling the bone into place with the scout's aid—though the brave winced a little at the crude surgery—he soon had the forearm set and was rewarded with a single guttural, "Wa-sha-ta-la!" from the stalwart warrior, which, Bob explained, meant, "Heap good."

Sitting afterward by the camp-fire, Scott and Iron Hand, since the young chief would not talk English, conversed in the Sioux tongue, the scout translating freely for his younger companion, while the squaws dressed the second antelope and cut it up for convenience in carrying on the horses to Casement's camp. Scott reserved only the hind-quarters of each animal for himself and Bucks, giving the rest to their hosts.

When it was late, Scott showed the boy how to pillow his head on his saddle and then stretched himself out to sleep. Bucks lay a long time looking up at the stars. When he fell asleep, he woke again very soon. His companion was sleeping peacefully beside him, and he saw Iron Hand sitting by the fire. Bucks easily imagined his arm would keep him awake. The squaws were still broiling pieces of antelope over the little blaze, which was neither bigger nor smaller than before, and together with the chief they were still eating. Bucks slumbered and woke again and again during the night, but always to see the same thing—

19

the three Indians sitting about the fire, broiling and eating the welcome and wholly unexpected venison.

CHAPTER IV

Before daybreak the scout roused his companion, and, after breakfast with the three Sioux, who, according to Bob, were still eating supper, the two hunters left their chance companions in the canyon, rode rapidly south, and, with their antelope haunches as trophies, reached Casement's camp about ten o'clock.

Stanley, who was conferring with Casement, came out of the tent greatly amazed at his scout's venturing so far on a hunt as to expose himself and his companion to danger.

"We were safe every minute, colonel," declared Scott.

"Safe?" echoed Stanley incredulously. "No man is safe, Bob, a mile from the track-layers. The Sioux killed and scalped one of our engineers not ten miles from here, when we were running this very line last winter."

"This lad," nodded Scott, "is as good a shot as I am. He brought down the first antelope. We get along with the Sioux all right, too, don't we, Bucks?" he demanded, appealing to his fellow-hunter. "We ate supper with them last night," he added to mystify his listeners, "and camped with Iron Hand."

Even General Casement stared at this and waited to hear Scott tell Stanley the story of their night's adventure. "However, colonel," concluded Scott, "there is a war party of Cheyennes near here. It is a good time to be careful."

"All right, Bob," retorted Stanley, looking at his scout keenly, though no one could be angry at Scott long. "You set the example."

The words were hardly out of his mouth when an operator came running down the track from the telegraph tent with a message for General Casement. It contained word from the operator at Peace River that section men reported a war party of Indians, crossing the railroad near Feather Creek, had attacked an emigrant party camped there.

In an instant the whole construction camp had the news and the work was thrown into confusion. Feather Creek was twenty miles away. Orders flew fast. A special train was made up, and Stanley taking command, with Casement to aid, made ready instantly to leave for the scene of the disaster.

The men running from the grade fell into line like veteran soldiers. Indeed, most of them had seen service in the war just closed and the smell of powder was no novelty. Bob Scott turned the venison over to Oliver and loaded his horse in the car with those of the cavalrymen. Under Stanley's orders he himself rode as pilot in the cab with the engine crew. Bucks also reported to Stanley, and within twenty minutes the relief train carrying two hundred men was plunging down the long hill toward Feather Creek. Heads were craned out of the car windows, and in rounding every curve Bucks, with the scout Leon Sublette, sitting greatly wrought up behind Stanley and Casement, expected momentarily to see Cheyenne war bonnets spring up out of the stunted cedars that lined the hills along the right of way.

But not a sign could be seen of any living thing. The train reached Feather Creek, and slowly crossed the bridge before Scott signalled the engineman to stop. His eye had detected the scene of the fight, and the ground beyond—a low cut—was favorable for getting the men safely out of the cars.

As the engine slowed, a little scene of desolation beside the right of way met Bucks's eye, and he caught sight of the ghastly battle-field. A frightened section crew emerged from the wild-plum thickets along the creek bottom, as the cavalrymen, followed by Casement's armed men, poured out of the three cars. Stanley with his scouts led the way to the emigrant camp, where the fight had taken place. The wagons had been burned, the horses run off, and the three unfortunate men butchered.

Bucks experienced a shock when Scott came upon the three dead men whose mutilated bodies had been dragged from the scene by the section men and who lay with covered faces side by side under a little plum-tree, fragrant with blossoms and alive with the hum of bees. The sunshine and the beauty of the spot contrasted strangely with the revolting spectacle upon the grass.

Stanley gave the orders by which the bodies were conveyed to the train and with the scouts and cavalrymen reconnoitering the surrounding country, Casement's men lay on their arms in the shade of the cut. Dancing rigged a pony instrument to the telegraph wires, which had not been disturbed, and Bucks transmitted messages to Fort Kearney advising the commanding officer of the murders and adding afterward the report of Scott and Sublette as to the direction the marauders had taken in flight.

"Who were the beasts, Bob, that could treat men like that?" demanded Bucks in an angry undertone, when he had clicked the messages over the wires.

"Bad Indians," answered Scott sententiously. "You have that kind of white men, don't you? These fellows are probably Turkey Leg's thieving Cheyennes. We shall hear more of them."

In the meantime the scouts and the cavalry detail rode out again trying to unmask the Cheyennes, but without success. It was a week before they were even heard of, and after an all-day attempt to do something, the train backed up to camp and work was resumed as if nothing had happened.

After waiting a few days, Stanley, always restive under idleness, determined to push on across the Sweet Grass country with horses, to learn how the timber cutters on the river were faring with their slender military guard. The party, consisting of the detail of ten men and the two scouts and Bucks, started one morning at sunrise and made their way without molestation into the little-known mountain range called then, as far south as Colorado, the Black Hills.

Stanley explained to Bucks during the morning how the chief engineering difficulty of the whole transcontinental line confronted the engineers right where they were now riding. Here the mountains were thrown abruptly above the plain to a great height and the locating engineers were still at their wits' ends to know how to climb the tremendous ascent with practicable grades. Stanley became so interested in studying the country during the day, as the difficulties of the problem presented themselves afresh to him, that the party made slow progress. Camp was pitched early in the afternoon under a ridge that offered some natural features for defence. Here the cavalrymen were left, and Stanley, taking Scott, started out after some venison for supper. Bucks stood by, looking eager as the two made ready for the hunt.

"Come along if you like," said Stanley at length. "You won't be happy, Bucks, till you get lost somewhere in this country."

Sublette lent Bucks a rifle, and the three men set out together, riding rapidly into the rough hills to the northwest. Scott covered the ground fast, but he searched in vain for sign of antelope. "Indians have been all over this divide," he announced after much hard riding and a failure to find any game. "It doesn't look like venison for supper to-night, colonel. Stop!" he added suddenly.

His companions, surprised by the tone of the last word, halted. Leaning over his pony's neck the scout was reading the rocky soil. He dismounted, and walking on, leading his horse, he inspected, very carefully, the ground toward a dry creek bed opening to the east.

He was gone perhaps five minutes. "Colonel," he said, smiling reassuringly, when he returned, "this is no place for us."

"Indians," said Stanley tersely.

"Cheyennes. Back to camp."

"Down the creek?" suggested Stanley.

"The bottom is alive with Indians."

"Up then, Bob?"

"Their camp is just above the bend. They have spotted our trail, too, somehow. It may be they are riding easy to close in on us," smiled Scott, while Bucks's hair began to pull. "Our way out is over this divide." He indicated the rough country east of the creek as he spoke.

"Divide!" exclaimed Stanley, looking up at the practically sheer walls of rock that hedged the course of the creek. "We can't climb those hills, if we never get out."

"They're not quite so bad as they look. Anyway, colonel, we've got to."

"They can pick us off our horses like monkeys all the way up!"

"It's a chance for our scalps, colonel. And it will be as hard riding for them as it is for us."

Stanley looked at Bucks with perplexity. "This boy!"

"I can make it, Colonel Stanley," exclaimed Bucks, who felt he must say something.

Stanley still hesitated.

"We've no time to lose," smiled Scott significantly.

"Then go ahead, Bob."

They had half a mile of comparatively level ground to cross before they began their climb, and this strip they rode very hard. When they reached the hills, Scott headed for a forbidding-looking canyon and urged his horse without ceasing through the rocky wash that strewed its floor. Stanley, with an excellent mount, could have kept well up, but he had put Bucks ahead of him in the safe place of the little procession, and the boy had difficulty in keeping within call of their active leader. The minute they were out of sight of the creek bottoms, Scott, choosing an apparently unscalable ascent, urged his horse up one of the canyon walls and the three were soon climbing in order.

Happily, Bucks's scrub horse gave a better account of himself in climbing than he had done in covering better ground. As their horses stumbled hurriedly along the narrow ledges, they made noise enough to wake the Indian dead and the loose rock tumbled with sinister echoes down the canyon wall. But progress was made, and the white men felt only anxious lest pursuit should catch them exposed on the uncovered height up which they were fast clambering.

Secure in their escape, the three were nearing the coveted top when a yell echoed through the canyon from below. There was no mistaking such a yell. Bucks, who had never heard anything so ferocious, had no need to be told what it was—it, so to say, introduced itself. And it was answered by another yell, more formidable still, and again by a chorus of yells. Then it seemed to Bucks's unaccustomed ears as if a thousand lusty throats were opened, and scared rigid he looked behind him and saw the canyon below alive with warriors.

They were riding helter-skelter to reach a range where they could pick the fugitives off the crest of the canyon side. Within a minute, almost, their rifles were cracking. Scott had already reached a point of concealment, and above the heads of Bucks and Stanley fired his rifle in answer. An Indian brave, riding furiously to a rock that would have commanded Stanley and Bucks as they urged their horses on, started in his saddle as Scott fired and clutched his side instantly with his rifle hand. His pony bolted as the half-hitch of the rawhide thong on its lower jaw was loosened and the rider, toppling, fell heavily backward to the ground. The riderless horse dashed on. The yelling Indians had had their blunt warning and now scurried for cover. The interval, short as it was, gave Bucks and Stanley a chance.

Spurring relentlessly and crouching low on their horses' necks, they made a dash across the exposed wall of rock near the top, that lay between them and safety. A renewed yell echoed the rage and chagrin of their pursuers, and a quick fire of scattering shots followed their rapid flight, but the Indians were confused, and Bucks, followed by his soldier champion, flung himself from his saddle in the clump of cedars behind which Scott, safely hidden, was reloading his rifle. Choosing his opportunity carefully, Stanley fired at once at an exposed brave and succeeded in disabling him. Bucks was forbidden to shoot and told to hold his rifle, if it were needed, in readiness for his companions. With the bullets cutting the twigs above their heads, Stanley and Scott held a council of war. Scott insisted on remaining behind to check their pursuers where they were, while the two with him rode on to safety.

"I can hold this bunch, colonel," declared Scott briefly. "There may not be a second chance as good. Get on with the boy before another party cuts you off. They can cross below us and save two or three miles. Get away."

"But how will you get away?" demanded Bucks.

Stanley laughed. "Never mind Bob. He could crawl through a Cheyenne village with a camp-fire on his back. It's what to do with you, Bucks, that bothers us."

"Just you get on, colonel," urged Bob. "I'll manage all right. Leave your horse," he added, turning to Bucks, "and you take mine."

Bucks protested and refused to leave Scott with an inferior mount, but his protests were of no avail. He was curtly directed by Stanley to do as he was told, and unwillingly he turned his horse over to Scott and took the scout's better steed. Scott added hurried and explicit directions to Stanley as to the course to follow back to camp, and without loss of time Stanley and Bucks crouching behind friendly rocks led their horses up the inner canyon wall and, remounting at the top, galloped hurriedly down a long ridge.

At intervals, shots from the Indians reached their ears, and long-drawn yells, followed by the sharper crack of Scott's rifle, echoed from the west as the scout held the wall against the enemy. Bucks did not understand the real danger that the scout feared for his party. It was that other parties of the marauding Cheyennes might, by following the creek, gain the divide in time to cut off the railroad men from their line of escape. The sounds of the stubborn contest behind them died away as their straining horses gradually put miles between them and the enemy. The fugitives had reached the summit of the hills and with a feeling of safety were easing their pace when Bucks discerned, almost directly ahead of them, dark objects moving slowly along the foot of a wooded hill. The two men halted.

CHAPTER V

"Indians," announced Stanley after a brief moment of inspection.

"We are cut off," he added, looking alertly over the landscape about them. "This way, Bucks. Ride as low as you can." Without further words he made an abrupt turn to the right, striking south to get behind a friendly butte that rose half a mile away.

"The question now is," said Stanley, as they held their horses up a little after getting somewhat farther out of sight, "whether they have likewise seen us."

The harried pair were not long in doubt. They had hardly changed their course when there was immediate activity on the hill-side. The railroad men spurred on; the distant horsemen, now on their flank, dashed out upon the broad slope that lay between the two parties and rode straight and hard after the fleeing men. Stanley steadied his inexperienced companion as the latter urged his horse.

"Not too hard just now. Your pony will need all his wind. It's a question of getting away with our scalps and we must be careful. Follow me."

Bucks's heart, as he looked back, crowded up into his throat. A long skirmish line of warriors had spread across the unbroken plateau to the east, and Stanley, with nothing but instinct for a guide, was making at top speed to the south to get away from them.

As the two dashed on, they found to their consternation that the country was growing smoother and affording fewer hiding-places from the sharp eyes behind them. Stanley knew they must either ride through the hills ahead or perish. He sought vainly for some break in the great black wall of low-lying mountains toward which they were riding, yet from what he knew of the country he hardly dared hope for one.

He had reconnoitred these hills time after time when running the railroad lines and knew pretty well where he was. The pursuers, too, apparently sure of their prey, rode hard, gradually lessening the distance that separated them from the wary soldier and his companion. The Indians had ceased yelling now. It was beyond that. But even in his excitement and fear the inexperienced boy could not but admire the composure and daring of his companion.

As Stanley glanced now and again back at his enraged enemies he was every inch a soldier. And he watched the distance between the Cheyennes and himself as coolly as if calculating a mere problem in geometry. While saving every possible breath for his horses, he yet managed to keep the Cheyennes at a distance. The Indians, bent on overhauling the fleeing men before they could reach even the scant protection of the scattered timber they were now approaching, redoubled their efforts to cut off the escape.

Forced by the desperation of his circumstances, Stanley bent more and more to the west of south, even though in doing so he seemed to be getting into a more hopeless country. The veteran campaigner eyed Bucks's horse carefully as he turned in his saddle, but Scott's wiry beast appeared quite fresh, and Stanley, turning his eyes, again swept the horizon for a friendly break in the black walls ahead. As he did so he was startled to see, directly in front, Indians riding at full speed out of the hills he was heading for. He reined his galloping horse and turned straight into the west.

"Bucks," he exclaimed, looking with concern at the rider now by his side, "it's a case of obey orders now. If I stop at any time, you ride straight on—do you understand? You've got a revolver?" Bucks tapped the big Colt at his side. "Don't let them take you alive. And hold your last shot till a buck rides in for your scalp."

The straining horses seemed to understand the sharp words that passed from saddle to saddle. The Indians were already within gunshot, but too sure of their game to lose any time in shooting; nor was Stanley willing to waste a shot upon them. As he dodged in between a broken wall of granite and a scrubby clump of cedars, closely followed by Bucks, their pursuers could have picked either man from his saddle.

Stanley had no longer any fixed purpose of escape. He meant merely to dismount when he could ride no farther and sell his life as best he could, while Bucks took such further chance of escape as his companion's last stand might afford. The hard-driven fighter was even looking for a well-placed rock to drop behind, when the horse plunging under him lurched to one side of the cedars and a gulf in the walls suddenly opened before his surprised rider.

A rotten ledge of burned granite seemed to head a mountain wash directly in their path. There was a sheer drop of twenty feet to the crumbling slope of disintegrated stone under the head of the draw itself, but Stanley, without looking back, never hesitated. Urging his panting horse, he made a flying leap down into space, and horse and rider landed knee-deep in the soft, gravelly granite below them.

Bucks's mustang shied on the brink. He spurred him excitedly, and the trembling beast, nerving himself, leaped far out over the ledge, following Stanley so closely that he almost struck him with his hoofs as he went flying over the engineer's head. Bucks rolled headlong as his horse plunged into the loose débris. He scrambled to his feet and, spitting the gravel from between his bruised lips, caught the bridle of his horse as the latter righted himself.

No legs were broken and much was already gained.

"Quick!" cried Stanley. "Ride for your life!" he shouted as Bucks regained his saddle. The two spurred at the same time and dashed down the draw at breakneck speed just as the Indians yelling on the brink of the ledge stopped to pour a volley after the desperate men. Unable to land an effective shot, the Cheyennes, nothing daunted, and hesitating only a moment, plunged over the precipice after their quarry.

But they had lost their great advantage. The dry watercourse proved unexpectedly good riding for the fleeing railroad men. It was a downhill run, with their hopes rising every moment. Moreover, the draw soon turned sharply to the south and put a big shoulder of granite between the pursuers and the pursued. The horses of the latter were now relieved, and the wary Stanley, riding with some reserve speed, held his rifle ready for a stern shot should one become necessary. He found himself riding between two almost perpendicular walls washed by the same granite gravel into which they had plunged on the start, but with the course again turning, to his surprise, to the east. Once, Stanley checked the flight long enough to stop and listen, but the two heard the active Indians clattering down the canyon after them, and rode on and on.

As they could see by the lengthening shadow on the mountain-sides far above them, the sun was setting.

"Cheer up," cried Stanley, who had put his companion ahead of him. "We've got the best of them. All we need is open country."

He did not mention the chances of disaster, which were that they might encounter an obstacle that would leave them at bay before their tireless pursuers. Mile after mile they galloped without halting again to see whether they were being chased. Indeed, no distance seemed too considerable to put between them and the active war-paint in the saddles behind.

A new turn in the canyon now revealed a wide valley opening between the hills before them. Far below, golden in the light of the setting sun, they saw the great eastern slope of the Black Hills spreading out upon a beautiful plain.

Stanley swung his hat from his head with an exulting cry, and Bucks, without quite understanding why, but assuming it the right thing to do, yelled his loudest. On and on they rode, down a broad, spreading ridge that led without a break from the tortuous hills behind them into the open country far below. Stanley put full ten miles between himself and the canyon they had ridden out of before he checked his speed. The Indians had completely disappeared and, disappointed in their venture, had no doubt ridden back to their fastnesses to wait for other unwary white men. Stanley chose a little draw with good water and grass, and night was just falling as they picketed their exhausted horses and stretched themselves, utterly used up, on the grass.

"We are safe until morning, anyway," announced Stanley as he threw himself down. "And this Indian chase may be the luckiest thing that has ever happened to me in the troublesome course of an unlucky life.

"You don't understand," continued the engineer, wiping the sweat and dust from his tired face. Bucks admitted that he did not.

"No matter," returned his companion; "it isn't necessary now. You will sometime. But I think I have done in the last hour something I have been trying to do for years. Many others have likewise failed in the same quest."

Bucks listened with growing interest.

"Yes, for years," Stanley went on, "incredible as it may sound, I have been searching these mountains for just such a crevice as we have this moment ridden down. You see how this range"—the exhausted engineer stretched flat on his back, but, with burning eyes, pointed to the formidable mountain wall that rose behind them in the dusk of the western sky—"rises abruptly from the plains below. Our whole grade climb for the continental divide is right here, packed into these few miles. Neither I nor any one else has ever been able to find such a pass as we need to get up into it. But if we have saved our scalps, my boy, you will share with me the honor of finding the pass for the Union Pacific Railroad over the Rocky Mountains."

They were supperless, but it was very exciting, and Bucks was extremely happy. Stanley watched that night until twelve. When he woke Bucks the moon was rising and the ghostly peaks in the west towered sentinel-like above the plains flooded with silver. The two were to move at one o'clock when the moon would be high enough to make riding safe. It was cold, but fire was forbidden.

The horses were grazing quietly, and Bucks, examining his revolver, which he had all the time felt he was wretchedly incompetent to shoot, sat down beside Stanley, already fast asleep, to stand his watch. He had lost Sublette's rifle in falling into the wash-out. At least he had found no leisure to pick it up and save his hair in the same instant, and he wondered now how much he should have to pay for the rifle.

When the sun rose next morning the two horsemen were far out of the foot-hills and bearing northeast toward camp—so far had their ride for life taken them from their hunting ground. They scanned the horizon at intervals, with some anxiety, for Indians, and again with the hope of sighting their missing guide. Once they saw a distant herd of buffalo, and Bucks experienced a shock until assured by Stanley that the suspicious objects were neither Cheyennes nor Sioux.

By nine o'clock they had found the transcontinental telegraph line and had a sure trail to follow until they discovered the grade stakes of the railroad, and soon descried the advance-guard of the graders busy with plough and shovel and scraper. As they rode into camp the very first man to emerge from Casement's tent, with his habitual smile, was Bob Scott.

Casement himself, who had heard Scott's story when the latter had come in at daybreak, was awaiting Stanley's return with anxiety, but this was all forgotten in the great news Stanley brought. Sublette and Scott now returned to the hunting camp for the cavalry detail, and, reinforced by these, the two heroes of the long flight rode back to reconnoitre their escape from the mountains. Bucks rode close to Bob Scott and learned how the scout had outwitted his assailants at the canyon, and how after they had all ridden out of it, he had ridden into it and retraced with safety in the night the path that the hunters had followed in riding into the hill country.

The second ride through the long defile, which itself was now the object of so much intense inspection, Bucks found much less exciting than the first. The party even rode up to where the first flying leap had been made, and to Bucks's joy found Sublette's rifle still in the wash; it had been overlooked by the Indians.

What surprised Bucks most was to find how many hours it took to cover the ground that Stanley and he had negotiated in seemingly as many minutes.

CHAPTER VI

After a week in Casement's camp, Stanley and his cavalrymen, accompanied by Dancing, Scott, and Bucks, struck north and east toward the Spider Water River to find out why the ties were not coming down faster. Rails had already been laid across the permanent Spider Water Bridge—known afterward as the first bridge, for the big river finished more than one structure before it was completely subdued—and the rail-laying was hampered only by the lack of ties.

The straggling bands of Cheyennes had in the interval been driven out of the foot-hills by troops sent against them, and Stanley and his little escort met with no trouble on his rapid journey.

Toward evening of the second day a broad valley opened on the plain before them, and in the sunset Bucks saw, winding like a silver thread far up toward the mountains, the great stream about which he had already heard so much. Camp was pitched on a high bluff that commanded the valley in both directions for many miles, and after supper Scott and Bucks rode down to the river.

In its low-water stage nothing could have looked more sluggish or more sleepily deceptive than the mighty and treacherous stream. Scott and his companions always gave the river the name the Sioux had long ago given it because of its sudden, ravening floods and its deadly traps laid for such unwary men or animals as trusted its peaceful promise and slept within reach of its cruel power.

Standing in the glow of the evening sky in this land where the clear, bright light seemed to lift him high above the earth, Bucks looked at the yellow flood long and thoughtfully—as well he might—for the best of his life was to be spent within ken of its flow and to go in doing battle with it himself, or in sending faithful men to its battling, sometimes to perish within its merciless currents.

Next morning as the party, following a trail along the bluffs, rode up in the direction of the contractors' camps they discerned out on the river bottom a motley cluster of tents and shanties pitched under a hill. A number of flatboats lay in the backwater behind the bend and a quantity of ties corded along the bank indicated a loading-place, but no one seemed to be doing any loading. The few men that could be seen in the distance appeared to be loafing in the sunshine along the straggling street-way that led to the river. Stanley checked his horse.

"What place is that?" he demanded of Scott.

"That," returned the guide, "is Sellersville."

"Sellersville," echoed Stanley. "What is Sellersville?"

"Sellersville is where they bring most of the ties for the boats."

"Have they started a town down there on the bottoms?"

"They have started enough saloons and gambling dens to get the money from the men that are chopping ties."

Stanley contemplated for a moment the ill-looking settlement. A mile farther on they encountered a number of men following the trail up the river.

A small dog barked furiously at the Stanley party as they came up, and acted as if he were ready to fight every trooper in the detail. He dashed back and forth, barking and threatening so fiercely that every one's attention was drawn to him.

Stanley stopped the leader and found he was a tie-camp foreman from up-river taking men to camp. "Is that your dog?" demanded Stanley, indicating the belligerent animal who seemed set upon eating somebody alive.

"Why, yes," admitted the foreman philosophically. "He sort o' claims me, I guess."

"What do you keep a cur like that around for?"

"Can't get rid of him," returned the foreman. "He is no good, but the boys like his impudence. Down, Scuffy!" he cried, looking for a stick to throw at his pet.

Bucks surveyed the company of men. They were a sorry-looking lot. The foreman explained that he had dragged them out of the dens at Sellersville to go back to work. When remonstrated with for the poor showing the contractors were making, the foreman pointed to the plague-spot on the bottoms.

"There's the reason you are not getting any ties," said he lazily. "We've got five hundred men at work up here; that is, they are supposed to be at work.

29

These whiskey dives and faro joints get them the minute they are paid, and for ten days after pay-day we can't get a hundred men back to camp."

The foreman as he spoke looked philosophically toward the canvas shanties below. "I spend half my time chasing back and forth, but I can't do much. They hold my men until they have robbed them, and then if they show fight they chuck them into the river. It's the same with the flatboat men." He turned, as he continued, to indicate two particularly wretched specimens. "These fellows were drugged and robbed of every dollar they brought here before they got to work at all."

Stanley likewise gazed thoughtfully upon the cluster of tents and shacks along the river landing. He turned after a moment to Scott. "Bob," said he, looking back again toward the river, "what gang do you suppose this is?"

Scott shook his head. "That I couldn't say, Colonel Stanley."

"Suppose," continued Stanley, still regarding the offending settlement, "you and Dancing reconnoitre them a little and tell me who they are. We will wait for you."

Scott and the lineman swung into their saddles and started down the trail that led to the landing. Stanley spoke again to the foreman. "Can those men use an axe?" he demanded, indicating the two men that the foreman asserted had been robbed.

"They are both old choppers—but this gang at Sellersville stole even their axes."

"Leave these two men here with me," directed Stanley as he watched Scott and Dancing ride down toward Sellersville. "I may have something for them to chop after a while."

The foreman assented. "I don't like the bunch," he murmured; "but nobody at our camp wants to tackle them. What can we do?"

While the foreman continued to talk, Stanley again looked over the human wrecks that he had rounded up and brought out of Sellersville. "What can we do?" echoed Stanley, repeating the last question tartly. "Well, I'll tell you one thing we can do. We can throw Sellersville into the river."

Dancing and Scott were gone half an hour. The report, when they returned, was not encouraging. "It is a bunch of cutthroats from Medicine Bend, colonel," said Bob Scott.

"All friends of yours, I presume, Bob," returned Stanley.

The scout only smiled. "John Rebstock is there with his following. But the boss, I think, is big George Seagrue. He is mean, you know. George has got two or three men to his credit."

"Are we enough to clean them out, Bob?" inquired Stanley impatiently.

Scott looked around and his eye rested for a moment on Dancing. He hitched his trousers. "There's about thirty men down there. I expect," he continued reflectively, "we can take care of them if we have to."

Stanley turned to the sergeant of his troopers. "Pitch a permanent camp, sergeant. There will be nothing to take us any farther up the river."

As Stanley gave the order Bucks noticed that Dancing winked at Scott. And without the meaning glances exchanged by the lineman and the scout, Bucks would have understood from Stanley's manner that he meant strong measures. Stanley sent a further message to the contractor, and the foreman, followed by his convoy of humanity, started on. The soldiers, foreseeing a lively scene, stripped their pack-horses and set at work pitching their tents.

Leaving four men in camp, the engineer, accompanied by his escort, rode down the bluffs and, striking a lumber road, galloped rapidly through the poplar bottom-lands toward the gamblers' camp. It was an early tour for human wolves to be stirring, and the invaders clattered into Sellersville before they attracted any attention.

A bugler, however, riding into the middle of the settlement, sounded a trumpet call, and at the unwonted notes frowsy, ill-shaped heads appeared at various shanty doors and tent-flaps to see what was doing. Stanley sent one man from door to door to notify the inmates of each shelter to pack up their effects and make ready to move without delay.

Five troopers were detailed to guard three gambling tents that stood together in the middle of the camp, each of these being flanked by smaller dens. Word was then passed to the gamblers and saloon-keepers to line up on the river front.

Stanley regarded the gathering crowd with a cold eye. Scott, who stood near Bucks, pointed out a square-shouldered man with a deep scar splitting one cheek. "Do you know that fellow, Bucks?" he asked in an undertone.

"No; who is he?"

"That is a Medicine Bend confidence man, Perry. Do you remember the woman you helped out with a ticket to Iowa? Perry is her husband—the man that Dave Hawk made pay up."

Perry was a type of the Sellersville crowd now being evicted. There was much talk as the soldiers urged and drove the gang out of one haunt after another and a good deal of threatening as the leaders marched out in front of Stanley.

"Who is running this camp?" demanded the officer curtly. The men looked at one another. A fat, slow-moving man with small blue eyes and a wheezy voice answered: "Why, no one in particular, colonel. We're just a-camping in a bunch. What's a-matter? Seagrue here," he nodded to a sharp-jawed companion, "and Perry," he added, jerking his thumb toward the scarred-faced man, "and me own these two big tents in partners."

"What's your name?"

"My name's Rebstock."

"Produce the axes stolen here from these two men," said Stanley, indicating the choppers behind him. There was a jangle of talk between Rebstock and his associates, and Perry, much against his inclination, was despatched to hunt up the axes. It was only a moment before he returned with them.

Rebstock, with a show of virtue, reprimanded Perry severely for harboring the men that had stolen the axes. "Sorry it happened, colonel," he grumbled, after he had abused the thieves roundly in a general way, "and I'll see it doesn't happen again. We can't watch everybody in a place like this. Tell your men," he continued, expanding his chest, "to leave their axes with me when they come to Sellersville—what?"

The assurances were lost on Stanley. "Rebstock," said he, in a tone that Bucks had not heard before from him, "take your personal effects, all of you—and nothing else—and load them on a flatboat. I will give you one hour to get-out of here."

Rebstock almost fell over backward. He wheezed in amazement. There was an outburst of indignant protests. A dozen men clamored at once. Perry rushed forward to threaten Stanley; others cursed and defied him.

"Who are you, and what do you mean giving orders like that?" demanded Seagrue, confronting him angrily.

"No matter who I am, you will obey the orders. And you can't take any tents or gambling apparatus or liquors. Pack up your clothes and camp stuff—nothing else—and get out."

If a bombshell had dropped into Sellersville, consternation could not have been more complete. But it became quickly apparent that not all of the gang would surrender without a fight. The leaders retreated for a hurried consultation.

Rebstock walked back presently and confronted Stanley. "What's your law for this?" he demanded, breathless with anger.

Stanley pointed to the ground under their feet.

"What's your title to this land, Rebstock? It belongs to the railroad that those ties belong to. Where is your license from the United States Government to sell whiskey here? You are trespassers and outlaws, with no rights that any decent man ought to respect. You and your gang are human parasites, and you are going to be stripped and sent down the river as fast as these flatboats will carry you."

Without waiting for any rejoinder, Stanley turned on his heel and walked away, leaving Rebstock speechless. The threats against the intruders continued, but Stanley paid no attention to any of them. Scott and the five troopers faced the gamblers. Stanley called to the two wood-choppers, who stood near with their axes, and pointed to the gambling tents.

"Chop up every wheel and table in there you can find," said he.

A cry went up from Perry when he heard the order, but the axemen, nothing loath, sprang inside to their work, and the crashing of the gambling furniture resounded through the alarmed camp. Stanley made no delay of his peremptory purpose. The tent attacked belonged to Seagrue, who, common report averred, feared nothing and nobody, while the gambling implements were Perry's.

Seagrue rushed to his property, revolver in hand. Bill Dancing, who stood at Stanley's side, stepped into his way.

"Hold on, Seagrue," he said. The gambler, fully as large a man as Dancing, faced his opponent with his features fixed in rage. "Get away," he shouted, "or I will knock your head off."

All eyes centred on the two men. Every one realized that open war was on and that it needed only a spark to start the shooting. The gamblers, rallying to Seagrue, backed him with oaths and threats.

"Seagrue, put down that pistol or I'll wring your neck," returned the lineman, baring his right arm as he sauntered toward the outlaw. Bucks, beside Stanley, stood transfixed as he watched Dancing. The lineman's revolver was slung in the holster at his side.

Seagrue hesitated. He saw Bob Scott standing in the doorway of the gambling tent with his rifle lying carelessly over his arm. He was actually covering Seagrue where he stood—and Seagrue knew that Bob Scott was deadly with a rifle. But Dancing was walking directly up to him and Seagrue dared not be shamed before his own associates. He jumped back to fire, but it was too late.

Dancing caught his wrist. Both were men of great strength, and their muscles knotted as they grappled. It was only after a moment that the lineman could be seen to gain. Then, as he bent the gambler's arm back, he suddenly released it and struck the revolver out of his hand. Seagrue, with a curse, sprang back, and drawing a knife rushed for the second time at the lineman. Dancing jumped to one side. As he did so he seized an axe from the hand of one of the choppers and turned again on Seagrue. The gambler made a lunge at his throat, but as he threw himself forward, Dancing, springing away, brought the axe around like a flash and laid it flat across his assailant's forearm. The knife flew twenty feet, and before the gambler could recover himself the railroad man with one hand like a vice on his throat bore him to the ground.

"Give me a piece of rope," muttered Dancing as Stanley ran up.

IT WAS ONLY AFTER A MOMENT THAT
THE LINEMAN COULD BE SEEN TO GAIN.

Bob Scott slashed a tent guy and handed it to him. In another minute Dancing, in spite of Seagrue's struggles, had lashed his prisoner hand and foot. Picking him up bodily, he walked unopposed to the landing, and to the astonishment of the spectators heaved Seagrue with scant ceremony into a flatboat. There a trooper kept him quiet. Walking back, the lineman brushed the dust of the encounter from his arms as if to invite any further Sellersville champion to come forward. But John Rebstock, the really responsible head of the place, showed no desire to meet Dancing, and Perry, the sneak of the trio, only ranted while Rebstock stood at a respectable distance wheezing his surprise at the tremendous exhibition of strength. And the work of destruction went forward.

Adjoining the Seagrue tent stood a saloon in which the men were now ordered to demolish the stock. This renewed the excitement among Rebstock's followers.

"Don't waste any time," was Stanley's order. "They may rush us. Knock in the head of a keg of whiskey, pour it over the bar, and burn the shanty."

The gamblers were, in fact, mustering for a charge on the invaders. Before they could act the saloon was ablaze and the flames, rising amid the yells and execrations of its owners, leaped to the big tent adjoining. In front of this the soldiers in a skirmish line held back the scurrying outlaws. Within a few moments Sellersville was ablaze from end to end and its population, including Perry and Rebstock, driven to the flatboats, were floating with threats and curses down the muddy current of the Spider Water.

CHAPTER VII

Stanley's next camp was pitched down the river where the overland telegraph line crossed the Spider Water, and Bucks, installed in a smart army tent with a cracker-box for a stool and a packing-case for an instrument table, was, through Dancing's efforts, put in communication by wire with Medicine Bend and the west country as far as Sleepy Cat, where the War Department was establishing an army post.

Stanley, with Bob Scott, now spent a great deal of time in the saddle between the bridge and the upper tie-camps, and his presence made itself felt in the renewed energy everywhere apparent among the contractors and their men. Bucks, chained to a wire, as he expressed it, found the days dragging again and would much rather have been at liberty to ride with Scott, who, when free, hunted in the foot-hills.

One day Bucks was sitting alone in his tent, looking for the hundredth time over a worn copy of *Harper's Weekly* that he had picked up at Casement's camp, when a dog put his nose in the tent door. A glance revealed merely a disconsolate, unpromising cur, yet Bucks thought he had seen the dog before and was interested. He seemed of an all-over alkali-brown hue, scant of hair, scant of tail, and with only melancholy dewlap ears to suggest a strain of nobler blood in an earlier ancestry. He looked in with the furtive eye of the tramp, and as if expecting that a boot or a club would most probably be his welcome.

But Bucks at the moment was lonely—as lonely as the dog himself—and as the two fixed their eyes intently on each other, Bucks remembered that this was the tie foreman's dog, Scuffy.

Scuffy had appeared at the psychological moment. Bucks regarded him in silence, and the dog perceiving no immediate danger of assault stood, in silence, returning Bucks's stare. Then watching the boy's eye carefully, the dog cocked his head just the least bit to one side. It was a mute appeal, but a moving one. Bucks continued, however, his non-committal scrutiny, recalling that the foreman had said nothing good of Scuffy, and the homeless cur stood in doubt as to his reception. But realizing, perhaps, that he had nothing to lose and everything to gain, the little vagabond played his last card—he wagged his stubby tail.

A harder heart than Bucks's might have been touched. The operator held out his hand. No more was needed; the melancholy tramp stepped cautiously forward waving his alert flag of truce. He sniffed long and carefully as he neared Bucks, looked solicitously into the boy's eyes, and then smelt and licked the proffered hand. It was a token of submission as plainly expressed as when Friday, kneeling, placed Robinson Crusoe's foot on his head. Bucks reached into a paper bag that Bill Dancing had left on the table and gave the dog a cracker.

Scuffy snapped up the offering like one starving. A second cracker and a third disappeared at single gulps. For the length of the dog, the size of his mouth appeared enormous. In a moment the cracker-bag was emptied and Scuffy again licked the friendly hand. It did not take Bucks long to decide what to do. In another moment he had resolved to adopt his tramp visitor. The day happened to be Friday, and Bucks at once renamed him Friday. When Dancing, who had been with Bob Scott hunting, came in late that night he found Bucks asleep and Scuffy lying in Dancing's own bed, from which he was ejected only after the most vigorous language on his own part as well as on that of the lineman. Even then, Scuffy retreated only as far as Bucks's feet, where he slept for the rest of the night undisturbed.

"Where did he come from?" growled Dancing in the morning as he sat with his pipe regarding the intruder, who acted quite at home, with a critical eye.

Bucks explained that this was the tie foreman's runaway dog, Scuffy, and beyond Scuffy's first appearance at the tent door he could tell him nothing. Scuffy simply and promptly assumed a place in camp and Bucks became, willy-nilly, his sponsor. But his effort to rename him came to nothing. Scuffy gave no heed when called "Friday," but for "Scuffy" he sprang to attention instantly.

Bill Dancing decided, off-hand, that "the pup" was worthless. Scott, whose smile was kindly even when sceptical, only corrected Bill to the extent of saying that Friday or Scuffy, whoever or whatever he might be, was no pup; that he was a full-grown dog and in Bob's judgment he would need no guardian.

One day, shortly after Scuffy had been put upon the pay-roll, Scott came in from a trip after venison with word that there were black bears in the hill canyons. The thought of bear's meat aroused every one, and Stanley suggested a bear hunt. Scott had to send down to Stanley's ranch at Medicine Bend for his dogs and some delay followed. But when the three hounds arrived there was excitement enough to compensate for it. One of the dogs was a big black fellow and his companions were brown full-bloods. The hounds, one and all, set on Scuffy the moment they reached camp, and it was only by the most dexterous manœuvres that the strange dog escaped being eaten alive. Indeed, Bob Scott remarked at once that if Scuffy should survive the greetings of his new comrades he would prove his right to live. The hounds always set upon him at meal-times, usually chewed him at bed-time, and harried him at all times.

To a less hopeful temperament than Scuffy's, life would not have seemed worth living. It was only Bucks who insured him anything at all to eat, and the enmity of the big, rangy hounds for the lean and hungry tramp dog left him no peace save when they were fighting in dreams. To accept life under such conditions indicated that Scuffy was a philosopher, and he accepted the conditions cheerfully, filching what he could of sustenance from the common pot and licking his troublesome wounds at night after his truculent companions had gone to sleep.

As soon as the tie-supply trouble had been lessened Stanley took things more leisurely and the interval afforded the opportunity for the delayed bear hunt. Bob Scott and Dancing were to go with Stanley, and Bucks being freed for one day from his key was invited to be of the party. All hands were in the saddle by daybreak, and Scott's hounds were baying and tearing around camp wild with excitement.

At the last moment a complication arose. Scuffy, who until the moment of starting had for prudential reasons—that is, to avoid being eaten up—remained in obscurity, joined the hunters. Every one in turn tried to drive him back, but long practice had made him expert in dodging missiles and had rendered him insensible to reproach. The hounds were too filled with the prospect of sport to pay any attention to Scuffy. In vain, Bob Scott tried to set them on him and drive him back to camp. On this occasion, when bullying would plainly have been justified, no hound would assail Scuffy. Bucks drove him again and again from the flank of the advance only to have the mortification of seeing him reappear a mile or two farther along the trail, and it was at last decided to leave him to his fate at the paw of a bear—which no one made doubt he was certain to suffer. At that moment Bucks and Bill Dancing, riding together, saw a deer frightened from a thicket running toward the river. Bucks jumped from his horse and lifted his rifle to take a shot, but by the time he was ready to fire the deer had vanished.

Led by Scott, the hunters rode at once into the rough country to the west, where in the mountain fastnesses the bears loved to feed. The hounds gave tongue vigorously, and Scuffy, who had by this time not only established himself but had impudently taken the lead and was heading the pack, barked loudest and longest.

"Did anybody ever see conceit equal to that?" demanded Stanley. "Look at that cur leading the hounds."

Bucks was mortified and expressed his regret.

"Don't mind him, Bucks," remarked Dancing consolingly. "That dog won't bother long. The first time the hounds run in, the bear will finish *him*."

Bucks did not know precisely what Bill meant by "running in," but he was not to be long in doubt. The pack struck a fresh trail almost at once and the hunters had a long ride along a mountain-side covered with fallen timber and cut by innumerable wash-outs that made the riding hard and dangerous. Scott found

37

intervals to encourage Bucks, whose youth and inexperience made his task of keeping up with the others a difficult one. "Take it easy," said Scott encouragingly as the operator tried to urge his mount.

"I am keeping you all back, Bob."

"Plenty of time. You are doing wonders for mountain-riding. When we close in on the bear don't be too keen to get near him. You wouldn't be safe for a minute on your horse if the dogs didn't keep the bear busy. As long as the dogs worry the bear you are safe. A bear will never chase a man as long as a dog keeps at him. It's only when the dogs refuse to go in any longer that the danger begins. When that happens, look out. Keep a respectful distance all the time and a road open behind you. That's all there is to a bear fight."

As he spoke, the hounds yelped sharply and Scott spurred forward. The hunters were threading a grove of quaking asp and the dogs had come up with the bear on an opening of shale rock surrounded by down timber. Throwing his reins and advancing cautiously on foot, Stanley, followed by his companions, who spread themselves in a wide semicircle, took his place, the others, as they best could, choosing their own.

The bear, a full-grown male, met the onset of the hounds with grim confidence. The dogs encircled him with a ring of ferocious teeth, running in from behind whenever they could to nip the huge beast in the haunches or on the flank. But the surprise of the encounter was Scuffy.

"Look," cried Bill Dancing, under whose wing Bucks had taken his post. "Look at him! Why, the pup is a world-beater!"

In truth, Scuffy was the liveliest and most impudent dog in the pack, and when the fight was fully on, managed to worry the angry bear more than the hounds did. Within a moment the black hound, over-bold, imprudently rushed the bear in front. A paw darting from the huge beast caught him like a trip-hammer and stretched him helpless. In that moment the bear exposed himself to Stanley's rifle and a shot rang across the mountain-side. Scott watched the result anxiously. But the slug instead of dropping the bear served only to enrage him. For an instant the two hounds lost their heads and the infuriated bear charged Bucks and Bill Dancing.

The shale opening became a scene of confusion. Exposing himself recklessly, Scott tried to urge the dogs forward, but they had lost their nerve. It needed only this to upset everything. The hunters closed in together, and the critical moment had come; deaf alike to command and entreaty, the two hounds refused to go in, and Scuffy, flying wildly about the bear, seemed unable to check him. Dancing stopped long enough to take one shot, and ran—with Bucks, who had found no chance to shoot, following. The bear gained fast on the long-legged lineman and his boy companion. A wash-out, hidden by a clump of bushes, lay directly in the path of flight. Dancing, perceiving it, dashed to the left and escaped. He shouted a warning to Bucks, who, not understanding, plunged straight over the declivity and sprawled into the wash-out with the bear after him. Catching his rifle, the boy scrambled to his feet with his pursuer less than twenty feet away. Between the two there was only open ground, and the bear was scrambling for Bucks when Scuffy sprang down the shale bank and confronted the enemy.

It looked like certain death for Scuffy, but the tramp dog did not hesitate. He rushed at the bear with a fury of snapping, though not without a lively respect for the sweep of the brute's fore paws. The little dog, freeing himself forever in that moment from the stigma of cur, put up a fight that astonished the big brute.

Scuffy raced at him first on one side and then on the other, bounding in and out like a rubber ball, dashing across his front and running clear around the circling bear, nipping even an occasional mouthful of hair from his haunches. He made noise enough for a pack of dogs and simulated a fury that gave the bear the surprise of his life. Bucks realized that only his four-legged friend stood between him and destruction and that so unequal a contest could not endure long. Skilful as the little fellow was, he was pitted against an antagonist quite as quick and wary. The clumsiness of the bear was no more than seeming, and any one of the terrific blows he dealt at Scuffy with his huge paw would have stretched a man lifeless. Bucks, collecting his disordered faculties, raised his rifle to help his champion with a shot. His heart beat like a hammer in his throat, but he knew there was only one thing to do, that was to get the rifle-sights carefully lined in his eye and shoot when Scuffy gave him an opening.

It came in a moment when the bear turned to smash Scuffy on his flank. Bucks fired. To his amazement, no result followed. The failure of the bear to show any sign of being hit stunned him, and he drew his revolver, never expecting to escape alive, when two shots rang across the wash as close together as if fired by the same hand. The bear sank like a falling tree. Yet he rallied and again rushed for Bucks, despite Scuffy's stout opposition and the yells from above, and finally halted only when Bob Scott, jumping into the wash-out, confronted him with a knife. There was an instant of apprehension, broken by a third shot from Dancing's rifle across the gully, and the bear crumpled lifeless almost at Scott's feet.

The scout turned to Bucks as he stood dazed by his narrow escape. Stanley, above, shouted. And Bill Dancing, carrying his empty rifle, and with his face bleeding from the briers, made his way down the opposite side of the wash. Scuffy, mounting the body of his dead foe, barked furiously.

The little dog was the real hero of the encounter. He had paid his keep and earned his way as a member of the family and as a bear-fighter. When Bucks picked up his rifle he told Scott of his bad miss in the critical moment of the fight. Bob took the gun from his hands and examined the sights good-naturedly. Bucks had neglected to change the elevation after he had aimed at the deer an hour earlier.

"Next time you shoot at a bear twenty feet away, don't leave your sights set for two hundred yards," was all Scott said.

CHAPTER VIII

The bruises that Bucks nursed were tender for some days, and Scott tried out some bear's grease for an ointment.

Scuffy, who had come out of the fight without a scratch, took on new airs in camp, and returned evil for evil by bullying the two wounded hounds who were too surprised by his aggressiveness to make an effective defence.

Bucks, when he was alone with the dog and time dragged heavily, turned for diversion to the only book in the camp, a well-thumbed copy of "The Last of the Mohicans." He had brought it with him to read coming out from Pittsburgh, and had thrown it into his bag when leaving Medicine Bend. In camp it proved a treasure, even the troopers, when they were idle, casting lots to get hold of it.

One day, when Bucks was absorbed in the romance, Bob Scott asked him what he was reading. Bucks tried to give him some idea of the story. Scott showed little apparent interest in the résumé, but he listened respectfully while cleaning his rifle. He made no comment until Bucks had done.

"What kind of Indians did you say those were," he asked, contracting his brows as he did when a subject perplexed him, "Uncas and Chingachgook?"

"Delawares, Bob. Know anything about Delaware Indians?"

Scott shook his head. "Never heard of Delawares in our country. I saw a Pottawottamie Indian once, but never any Delawares. Is this story about Uncas a true story?"

"As true as any story. Listen here." Bucks read aloud to him for a while, his companion at intervals asking questions and approving or criticising the Indian classic.

"If you could only read, Bob, you ought to read the whole book," said Bucks regretfully, as he put the volume aside.

"I can read a little," returned Scott, to Bucks's surprise. "All except the long words," added the scout modestly. "A man down at Medicine Bend tried to sell me a pair of spectacles once. They had gold rims, and he told me that a man with those spectacles could read any kind of a book. He thought I was a greenhorn," said the scout.

"Where did you learn to read?"

"A Blackrobe taught me."

Bucks held out the book. "Then read this, Bob, sure."

Scott looked at the worn volume, but shook his head doubtfully. "Looks like a pretty big book for me. But if you can find out whether it's true, I might try it sometime."

Stanley, after a few days, started up the river with Scott and Dancing, leaving his men in camp. Bucks, who was still too stiff to ride, likewise remained to receive any messages that might come.

There was an abundance of water-fowl in the sloughs and ponds up and down the river, and Bucks, the morning after Stanley's departure, leaving the troopers lounging in camp, started out with a shot-gun to look for ducks. He passed the first bend up-stream, and working his way toward a small pond thickly fringed with alders, where he had often seen teal and mallards, attempted to crawl within gunshot of it.

He was working his way in this fashion toward the edge of the water when he heard a clatter of wings and the next moment a flock of mallards rushed in swift flight over his head. He impulsively threw up his gun to fire but some instinct checked him. He was in a country of dangerous enemies and the thought of bears still loomed large in his mind. An instant's reflection convinced him that it was not his movement that had frightened the ducks, and he was enough of a hunter to look further than that for the cause. As caution seemed, from the soreness of his legs and arms, plainly indicated, he lay still to await developments.

Soon he heard a movement of trampling feet, and, seemingly, across the pond from him. Bucks thought of buffaloes. His heart beat fast at the thought of getting a shot at one until he reflected that he had no rifle. The next instant his heart stopped beating. Not ten feet from where he lay in the thick willows, an Indian carrying a rifle, and in war-paint, stole noiselessly along toward the camp. No sooner had he disappeared than a second brave followed, and while Bucks was digesting this fright a third warrior, creeping in the same stealthy manner and almost without a sound, passed the staring boy; the appearance of a fourth and a fifth raised the hair on Bucks's head till he was almost stunned with fright, but he had still to count three more in the party, one more ferocious-looking than another, before all had passed.

What to do was the question that forced itself on him. He feared the Indians would attack the troopers in camp, and this he felt would be a massacre, since the men, not suspecting danger, would be taken wholly unawares. Should he fire his gun as a signal? It would probably bring the Indians back upon him, but the thought of allowing the troopers to be butchered was insupportable. His hammers were cocked and his finger was on one trigger when he considered how useless the alarm would be. The troopers knew that he had gone duck hunting. They would expect to hear him shoot and would pay no attention to it. To rush out after the Indians would only invite his instant death.

There seemed nothing he could do and a cold sweat of apprehension broke over him. But if he fired his gun he might, at least, surprise the Indians. The report of a gun in their rear would alarm them—since they knew nothing of his presence or his duck hunting and might take fright. Without more ado he fired both barrels one after the other, careful only to shoot low into the willows, hoping the smoke would not rise so quickly as to betray him before he could make a dash for a new hiding-place.

His ruse worked and he ran at top speed for twenty yards before he threw himself into a clump of cotton-woods close to the camp trail and began to reload. While he was doing so a shout came from the direction of the railroad bridge. Not until then did Bucks understand what the Indians were after. But had he not understood, he would have known a moment later when he heard a sharp exchange of shots toward the camp, heard the dogs barking furiously, and saw the Indians, now on their ponies, running the troopers' horses past him at a breakneck gallop. The Indians yelled lustily at the success of their raid, the stampeded horses dashed panic-stricken before them, and the braves shouted back in derision at the vain efforts of the troopers to stop them with useless bullets. Bucks's own impulse was to empty a charge of birdshot into the last of the fleeing warriors, but this he knew might cost him his life, and he resisted the temptation. When he was sure all were past he ran toward the bluffs, and gaining a little eminence saw the fleeing Indians, a dozen in all, making their way jubilantly up the river. At the camp the discomfited cavalrymen were preparing for a siege, and in their excitement almost shot Bucks as he hove in sight.

Bucks gave a good description of the marauders, and, following him up to the pond, six of the troopers attempted some pursuit. This, to unmounted men, was useless, as they well knew. Indeed, they used caution not to come unawares on any friends of the escaping braves that might have lingered behind.

Colonel Stanley returned in the morning to hear that his escort had been unhorsed. Bob Scott grinned at the cavalrymen as they told the story. He assured them that they had got off lightly, and that if Bucks's signals had not alarmed the little war-party they might have carried away scalps as well as horses.

"We shall be in luck if we don't hear more of those fellows," said he to Bucks afterward. There was now manifestly nothing to do but to go in, and later in the day a freight train was flagged and the whole party, with Scuffy and the hounds, returned to Casement's camp. Scott sent his dogs thence to the ranch in Medicine Bend, and at Bucks's urgent request Scuffy was sent with them to await his own return to head-quarters.

CHAPTER IX

The foray of the Indians at the Spider Water Bridge proved, as Bob Scott had feared, only a forerunner of active hostilities. Casement had already taken all necessary measures of defence. His construction camp was moved steadily westward, though sometimes inside the picket lines of troops, despite the warring Indians and the difficulties of his situation. Alarms, however, were continual and the graders, many of whom were old soldiers, worked at all times with their muskets stacked on the dump beside them. In the construction camp Bucks saw also many negroes, and at night the camp-fires of their quarters were alive with the singing and dancing of the old plantation life in the South.

While waiting for Stanley's inspection of the grading and track-laying, Bucks relieved at times the camp operator, whose principal business was the rushing of emphatic demands to Omaha for material and supplies.

During other intervals Bucks found a chance to study the system that underlay the seemingly hopeless confusion of the construction work. The engineers moving far in advance had located the line, and following these came the graders and bridge- and culvert-builders, cutting through the hills, levelling the fills, and spanning the streams and water-ways with trestles and wooden bridges, miles in advance of the main army. Behind these came Casement's own big camp with the tiemen, the track-layers, and the ballast gangs.

Every Eastern market was drawn upon for materials, and when these reached Omaha, trains loaded with them were constantly pushed to the front. The chief spiker of the rail gang, taking a fancy to Bucks, invited him to go out with the rail-layers one day, and Bucks took a temporary commission as spike-dropper.

To do this, he followed Dancing up the track past a long construction train in which the men lived. The big box-cars contained sleeping-bunks, and those men who preferred more air and seclusion had swung sleeping-hammocks under the cars; others had spread their beds on top of the cars. Climbing a little embankment, Bucks watched the sturdy, broad-shouldered pioneers. A light car drawn by a single, galloping horse was rushed to the extreme end of the laid rails. Before it had fairly stopped, two men waiting on either side seized the end of a rail with their trap and started forward. Ten more men, following in twos, at a run, lifted the two rails clear of the car and dropped them in place on the ties. The foreman instantly gauged them, the horse moved ahead, and thirty spikers armed with heavy mauls drove the spikes furiously and regularly, three strokes to the spike, into the new-laid ties. The bolters followed with the fish-plates, and while Bucks looked the railroad was made before his eyes.

The excitement of the scene was unforgettable. In less than sixty seconds four rails had gone down. The moment a horse-car was emptied it was dumped off one side of the track, and a loaded car with its horse galloping to the front had passed it. The next instant the "empty" was lifted back on the rails, and at the end of a sixty-foot rope the horse, ridden by a hustling boy, was being urged back to where the rails were transferred from the regular flat cars. The clang of the heavy iron, the continuous ring of the spike mauls, the shouting of the orders, the throwing of each empty horse-car from the track to make way for a loaded one, these things were all new and stimulating to Bucks. The chief spiker laughed when the young operator told him how fine it was. He asked Bucks to look at his watch and time the work. In half an hour Bucks looked at his watch again. In the interval the gang had laid eight hundred feet of track.

"I don't see how you can work so fast," declared Bucks.

"Do you know how many times," demanded the spiker, "those sledges have to swing? There are eighteen ties and thirty-six spikes to every rail, three hundred and fifty-two rails to every mile, and eighteen hundred miles from Omaha to San Francisco—those sledges will swing sixty-eight million times before the rails are full-spiked—they have to go fast."

The words were hardly out of the chief spiker's mouth when a cry of alarm rang from the front. Bucks, looking eagerly, saw in the west a cloud of dust. At the same time he saw the tie gang running in dozens for their lives from the divide where they were working toward the camp. The men beyond them on the grade had scrambled into the wagons, dumped any ties they might contain helter-skelter to the ground, and were clinging to the wagon boxes. In these, the drivers standing up, lashed their horses with whip and line for life, and death, while everywhere beside and behind them other men on foot were racing back to safety.

New clouds of dust rose along the grade from the flying wagon wheels, the horses tore madly on, and as the heavy wagons jolted over the loose stones, the fugitives, yelling with excitement and alarm and clinging to one another as they bounced up and down, looked anxiously behind.

There was no uncertainty as to the cause of the panic. "Indians!" was the cry everywhere. Every man in camp had dropped his working implement and was moving somewhere on the double-quick. Every one, it seemed to Bucks, was shouting and running. But above the confusion of the surprise and the babel of voices, Bucks heard the sharp tones of Jack Casement giving orders.

The old soldiers in the working gang needed no further discipline. The timid and the skulkers scurried for the box-cars and the dugouts. On the other hand, the soldiers ran for the dumps where the arms were stacked, and seizing their muskets hurried back and, trained for the emergency, fell into line under their foremen.

Casement, musket in hand, taking the largest company of men as they formed in fours behind him, started forward at the double-quick, yelling now for the moral effect, to protect the retreat of the wagons. The men, scattering as they reached the edge of the camp, dropped into every spot of shelter, and at the same moment Stanley, mounted and alive with the vim and fire of the soldier, led a smaller body of men rapidly back to guard the rear of the camp, deploying his little force about the box-cars and flat cars as they hastened on. In an instant the construction camp had become a fortress defended by a thousand men.

It was none too soon. Stirring the yellow plain with the fury of a whirlwind, a band of Sioux warriors rode the fleeing railroaders furiously down. They appeared phantom-like out of every slip and canyon, and rode full-panoplied from behind every hill. The horizon that had shown five minutes before only the burning sunshine and the dull glare of the alkali sinks, danced now with the flying ponies of the Indians, and the hills echoed with ominous cries.

Without a word of warning, the few fleeing men who had been working too far from camp to reach it in safety were mercilessly cut down. Their comrades under arms, with an answering cry of defiance poured a volley of cartridge balls into the thin, black circle that rode ever closer and closer to the muzzles of the muskets. Jack Casement and his brother Dan recklessly urged their men to the most advanced posts of defence, and from behind scrapers, wagons, flat cars, and friendly hillocks the railroad men poured a galling fire into their active foe.

The Indians, seeking with unerring instinct the weakest point in the defence, converged in hundreds upon the long string of box-cars that made up the construction train at the rear of the camp, where Stanley, extending his few men in a resolute skirmish line, endeavored to prevent the savages from scalping the non-combatant cooks and burning the sleeping-cars. Bucks saw, conspicuous in the attack, a slender Sioux chief riding a strong-limbed, fleet pony with a coat of burnished gold and as much filled with the fire of the fight as his master was. Riding hither and thither and swinging a long, heavy musket like a marshal's baton, the Sioux warrior, almost everywhere at once, urged his men to the fighting, and the fate of the few white men they were able to cut down or scalp before Stanley could cover the line of box-cars seemed to add vigor to their onslaught.

Stanley himself, attacked by ten braves for every man he could muster at that point with a gun, dashed up and down the old wagon roads along the right of way, a conspicuous target for the Indians. His hat, in the mêlée, had disappeared, and, swinging a heavy Colt's revolver, which the Indians shrank from with a healthy instinct of danger, he pressed back the hungry red line again and again, supported only by such musketry fire as the men crouching under, within, and between the box-cars could offer.

Wherever he rode his wily foes retreated, but they closed in constantly behind him, and one brave, more daring than his fellows, succeeded in setting fire to a box-car. A shout of triumph rose from the circling horsemen, but it was short-lived. Stanley, wheeling like a flash, gave chase to the incendiary. The Sioux rode for his life, but his pony's pace was no match for the springing strides of Stanley's American horse.

For an instant the attention of the whole fight in the rear of the camp was drawn upon the rash brave and his pursuer. Bucks, with straining eyes and beating heart, awaited the result. He saw Stanley steadily closing the gap that separated him from his fleeing enemy. Then the revolver was thrown suddenly upward and forward, and smoke flashed from the muzzle. The echo of the report had hardly reached Bucks's ears when the revolver, swung high again to balance the rhythm of the horse's flight, was fired again, and a third time, at the doomed man.

The Indian, bending forward on his horse, caught convulsively at his mane, then rising high in his seat plunged head-foremost to the ground, and his riderless horse fled on. His pursuer, wheeling, threw himself flat in his saddle to escape the fire bent upon him from behind as he rode back. At that moment Dan Casement and his men hurried up on the double-quick. With him came Bucks, who had secured a rifle and fallen in. Some men of the welcome reinforcement were set at putting out the fire. Others strengthened Stanley's scattered skirmish line.

Convinced by the determined front now opposed to him of the impossibility of rushing the camp, the Sioux chief gave the signal to retire.

As if the earth had opened to swallow them up, the warriors melted away, and as suddenly as the plain had borne them into life it now concealed their disappearance. In twenty minutes they had come and gone as completely as if they had never been. But in that short interval they had left death and consternation in their wake.

CHAPTER X

Stirred by the increasing boldness of the Indians, Stanley returned with his party to Medicine Bend to take further measures for the defence of the railroad men.

Bucks, when he reported to Baxter, the train despatcher, found new orders waiting for him. He was directed to take charge of the station at Goose Creek. The train did not leave till night, and Bucks took advantage of the interval to go uptown to make some necessary purchases of linen and clothing. On his way back to the station, with his package under his arm, he saw, on the edge of the broad sidewalk, Harvey Levake. Levake was standing near a wooden-Indian cigar-store sign, looking directly at Bucks as the latter walked toward him. The operator, nodding as he came up, asked Levake, without parley, whether he would give him the money for the express charges on the cartridges.

If Bucks had exploded a keg of powder on the sidewalk there could not have been a greater change in the outlaw's manner. He stared at Bucks with contempt enough to pierce the feelings of the wooden Indian beside which he stood.

"What's that?" he demanded, throwing his head menacingly forward.

Bucks repeated his request, but so mildly that Levake took additional umbrage at his diffidence.

"See here," he muttered in a voice beginning like a distant roll of thunder and gathering force and volume as he continued, "don't insult me."

Bucks ventured to urge that he intended no insult.

"Don't insult me!" bellowed Levake in violent tones.

Again Bucks attempted to protest. It was useless. Levake insisted with increasing wrath upon hugging the insult to himself, while Bucks struggled manfully to get it away from him. And as Levake's loud words did not attract as much attention up and down the street as he sought, he stamped about on the sidewalk. Bucks's efforts to pacify him made matters momentarily worse.

Meantime a crowd such as Levake desired had gathered and Bucks found himself a target for the outlaw's continued abuse, with nobody to take his part. Moreover, the expressions on the faces about him now made him realize his peril quite as much as anything in Levake's words. It was becoming painfully evident that the onlookers were merely waiting to see Levake shoot him down.

"No man in Medicine Bend can insult me and live," cried Levake, winding up a tirade of abuse. "I'm known from one end of this street to the other. Nobody can spread lies in it about me."

He drew and flourished a revolver as he spoke. None in the crowd interfered with so much as a word. But even before the outlaw had finished what he was saying, a man of medium size and easy manner elbowed his way quietly through the circle of spectators, and, taking Bucks by the arm, drew him back and faced Levake himself. It was Bob Scott.

"What's all this about, Levake?" demanded Scott gently.

46

Levake had no alternative but to turn his wrath upon the Indian scout. Yet those who knew him perceived that it was done without much stomach for the job. Instead of growing momentarily greater the violence of his abuse now grew steadily less, and the thunder in his tones rolled further and further from the subject.

Half-turning to Bucks, Scott laid his hand on his arm again. "Excuse me," said he, deliberately and quietly, "but you are wanted quick at the station. They are waiting for you. Go right along, will you?"

Only too glad to get away and comprehending Scott's ruse, Bucks exclaimed, "Why, of course, certainly," and stepping quickly into the crowd walked away.

Turning again to Levake, Scott made no effort to check the torrent of his words. In consequence, the gambler found himself embarrassed by the prospect of talking himself out. This would not have been so bad except that his circle of admirers would, when he stopped talking, expect him to do something and he was now at a loss to decide just what to do. To shoot down Bucks was rather a different matter from a pistol duel with Scott.

None of the street loafers about the two men knew Scott, nor did any of them know that Levake had a prudent respect for Scott's trigger. As for Scott himself, a smile of contempt gradually covered his face as he listened to Levake's outbreak. He only waited patiently for the moment, which he knew must come, when Levake should cease talking.

"Your tongue, Levake," returned Scott at last, "is longer than a coyote's. Why do you stand here and bellow about being insulted? What is all this noise about, anyway? These fellows," a contemptuous nod indicated the men standing around, "all know, if you don't. You've been talking loud so you could get a crowd together and advertise yourself by shooting an unarmed boy, haven't you?"

The desperado broke out in fresh denials and curses, but he feared the ridicule of the Indian would bring the laughter of his admirers down on him. Nor was he keen to try a pistol duel. He remembered too well the attack he had once headed on an emigrant train that Scott was guarding, and from which the outlaws with Levake had carried away some unexpected and unwelcome bullets.

Scott, now taunting Levake openly, stepped directly in front of him. But the latter waved him away. "I'll settle my differences with you when I'm ready," he muttered. "If that fellow," he added, indicating Bucks, who was making record time across the square, "behaves himself, I'll let this go. If he doesn't, I'll fill him full of lead."

"When you do," retorted Scott, "remember just one thing—that I'm going to fill you full, Levake. Don't forget that."

Scott stepped backward. The crowd parted to let him through and Levake walked sullenly toward the cigar store.

Bucks wiped the perspiration from his forehead when he reached the station and drew a long breath. He waited until Scott crossed the square and joined him. The Indian only laughed when Bucks tried to thank him. "It is nothing," he said, "you are getting experience. Only don't tackle that man again till you give me notice beforehand."

The next morning Bucks installed himself at Goose Creek.

Goose Creek was a mere operating point and besides the rough wooden station, with an attic sleeping-room for the operator, boasted only a house for the section crew—six men taken care of by a China boy cook. East of the station stood an old road ranch belonging to Leon Sublette. For this, freight was at times unloaded and an Indian trail to the south led through the sand-hills as far as the Arickaree country. North of the river greater sand-hills stretched as far as the eye could reach. The long, marshy stretches of the Nebraska River lost themselves on the eastern and the western horizon and at times clouds of wild fowl obscured the sun in their flight across the sky.

Dancing came down to the new station to complete the instalment of the instruments and this broke for a day or two the loneliness of the new surroundings. Indeed, there was hardly time to be lonely. The constant round of interest attending the arrival of trains with their long halts, visits from trappers living at the ranch who were always ready to talk, and occasional calls from friendly Pawnees from the south, together with abundance of time for hunting the geese and ducks, made the days go.

But one early summer morning Bucks woke to an adventure not upon his daily programme. He walked downstairs after dressing, and as he stepped out on the platform the sand-hills touched by the rising sun shone in the northwest like mountains of gold. Looking at them he saw to his surprise they were covered with black objects that appeared to be moving.

Indians were first in his mind, and in his alarm he ran all the way to the section-house where the foreman, after a hasty study of the hills, explained that the suspicious-looking objects were buffaloes.

This information only added to Bucks's excitement. The China boy cook, Lee Ong, at the section-house appeared equally stirred at the situation and, after running in and out of the kitchen with much fluttering of cue and clattering of wooden shoes, promised Bucks a buffalo steak for dinner if he would bring in a hindquarter.

By the time Bucks had finished breakfast the whole country to the north was black with buffaloes. For hours they poured over the divide to the delight of the astonished boy, and after a time he wired Baxter at Medicine Bend that a herd of at least one million buffaloes was crossing the railroad at Goose Creek. As the grave despatcher seemed not greatly excited by this intelligence, Bucks followed up the story at intervals with vivid details. A wag on the wire in Medicine Bend played upon his enthusiasm by demanding frequent bulletins, even going so far as to ask the names of the leading buffaloes in the herd. When he had got all the laughs possible for the office out of the youthful operator, he wired Bucks that if the herd should linger too long on the right-of-way he must notify them that they would be held as trespassers.

This message had hardly reached Goose Creek when the China boy came running into the telegraph office. His eyes were staring, and his face was greenish-white with fright. "Indians!" he exclaimed, running to Bucks's side and dashing back again to the west window.

Bucks sprang to his feet. "Where?"

Lee Ong pointed to the northern sand-hills. Riding the broad slopes that led toward the river, Bucks saw a long string of braves, evidently a hunting party. The cook, beside himself with fear, ran out of the station before Bucks could stop him.

"Hi there, Lee," cried the operator, running after him. "Where are the section men?"

"Gone," cried Lee Ong, not ceasing to run, "all gone!" He pointed, with the words, to the east.

"Tell them to bring the hand-car down here!"

"Too much gone," shouted Ong. "Omaha!"

"Lee! Stop! Where are you going?"

Lee stopped only long enough to throw his right arm and forefinger with an excited gesture toward the west.

"San Francisco, San Francisco!" he cried.

"Why, Lee," exclaimed Bucks running after him, "hold on! You are crazy! San Francisco is fifteen hundred miles from here." This information did not visibly move Ong. "Indian no good," he cried, pausing, but only long enough to wave both hands wildly toward the sand-hills. "San Francisco good. No some more cook here. Indian come too quick"—Ong with his active finger girdled the crown of his head in a lightning-like imitation of a scalping knife—"psst! No good for Ong!"

It would have seemed funny to Bucks if he had not been already frightened himself. But if the section men had fled with the hand-car it meant he would have to face the Indians. Lee Ong, running like mad, was already out of hearing, and in any event Bucks had no wish to imperil the poor China boy's scalp with his own.

He turned an anxious eye toward the sand-hills. Then realizing that on the platform he was exposing himself needlessly, he hastened inside to his key and called up Medicine Bend. It was only a moment, but it seemed to the frightened operator a lifetime before the despatcher answered. Bucks reported the Indians and asked if there were any freight trains coming that he could make his escape on.

The despatcher answered that No. , the local freight, was then due at Goose Creek and would pick him up and carry him to Julesburg if he felt in danger. Bucks turned with relief to the east window and saw down the valley the smoke of the freight already in sight. Never had a freight train looked so good to his eyes as it did at that moment. He hailed its appearance with a shout and looked apprehensively back toward the sand-hills.

The activity in that direction was not reassuring. The Indians, too, apparently had noticed the smoke of No. trailing on the horizon. A conference followed, illustrated by frequent pointing and violent gesticulating to indicate the coming train. Then with a sudden resolve the whole party rode rapidly out of the hills and down toward the railroad.

Bucks's heart misgave him as he watched. But the cotton-woods growing along the river hid the Indians from his eyes and he could not surmise what they were doing. The information all went to the despatcher, however, who, more experienced, scented serious mischief when Bucks's bulletins now came in.

"Watch close," he wired. "It looks as if they were going to attack the train."

The operator's anxiety rose with the intimation. He ran out of doors and down the track, but he could neither hear nor see a thing except the slow-moving train with the smoke puffing from the awkward, diamond-stack locomotive moving peacefully toward the cotton-woods that fringed the eastern shore of Goose Creek. The very silence seemed ominous. Bucks knew the Indians were hidden somewhere in the cotton-woods and felt that they could mean nothing but mischief. He ran back to his key and reported.

"They will surely attack No. ," he wired. "I will run across the bridge and warn them."

"Where are the Indians?" demanded the despatcher.

"In the timber across the creek. I am starting."

"Don't be an idiot," returned the despatcher, with an expression of Western force and brevity. "They will lift your hair before you get half-way to the train. Stick to your key as long as you can. If they start to cross the creek, leg it for the ranch. Do you get me?"

Bucks, considerably flurried, answered that he did, and the despatcher with renewed emphasis reiterated his sharp inquiry. "Do you understand, young fellow? If they start to cross the creek, leg it for the ranch or you'll lose your hair."

Bucks strained his eyes looking for a sign of movement across the bridge. The cotton-woods swayed gently in the light breeze, but revealed nothing of what they hid.

The freight train continued to crawl lazily along, its crews quite unconscious of any impending fate. Bucks, smothering with excitement and apprehension, saw the engine round the curve that led to the trestle approach of the bridge. Then the trees hid the train from his sight.

"What are they doing?" demanded the despatcher, growing apprehensive himself. An appalling crash from the woods electrified Bucks, and the key rattled fast.

"They have wrecked the train," he wired without an instant's hesitation. "I can hear the crash of cars falling from the trestle."

Before he could finish his message he heard also the screech of an engine whistle. The next instant the locomotive dashed out of the woods upon the bridge at full speed and with cries of disappointment and rage the savages rode out to the very bank of the creek and into the water after it. Bucks saw the sudden engine and thought at first that the train had escaped. The next moment he knew it had not. The engine was light: evidently it had passed in safety the trap laid for its destruction, but the cars following had left the rails.

If confirmation of this conclusion had been needed, it came when he ran out upon the platform as the engine approached. Bucks waved vigorous signals at it, but the ponderous machine came faster instead of slower as it neared the station, and, with Bucks vainly trying to attract the attention of the engineman or fireman, the locomotive thundered past at forty miles an hour.

He caught one glimpse through the tender gangway as the engine dashed by and saw both men in the cab crouching in front of the furnace door to escape the fancied bullets of the savages. Bucks shouted, but knew he had been neither seen nor heard, and, as the engine raced into the west, his best chance of escape from an unpleasant situation had disappeared almost before he realized it.

Each detail was faithfully reported to the despatcher, who answered at once.

"Relief train," he wired, "now making up with a hundred men. Hold on as long as you can, but take no chances. What are they doing? Can you see or hear them?"

"They are yelling so you could hear them a mile."

"Scout around a little," directed the despatcher, "but don't get caught."

Bucks scouted around the room a little, but did not venture this time farther than the windows. He was growing very nervous. And the Indians, unrestrained in their triumph, displayed themselves everywhere without concealment. Helpless to aid, Bucks was compelled to stand and see a fleeing white man, the brakeman of the doomed train, running for his life, cut down by the pursuers and scalped before his eyes.

The horror and savagery of it sank deeply into the boy's heart and only the realization of his utter inability to help kept him quiet. Tears of fury coursed down his cheeks as he saw in the distance the murdered man lying motionless on the sand beside the track, and with shaking fingers he reported the death to Medicine Bend.

"The relief train has started," answered the despatcher, "with Stanley, Scott, Sublette, Dancing, and a hundred men."

As the message came, Bucks heard shooting farther up the creek and this continued at intervals for some moments. It was sickening to hear, for it meant, Bucks surmised, that another trainman was being murdered.

Meantime the Indians that he could see were smashing into the wrecked merchandise cars and dragging the loot out upon the open prairie. Hats, clothing, tobacco, provisions, camp supplies of every sort, and musical instruments, millinery, boots, and blankets were among the plunder. The wearing apparel was tumbled out of the broken cases and, arrayed in whatever they could seize, the Indians paraded on their horses up and down the east bank of the creek in fantastic show.

Some wore women's hats, some crinoline hoop-skirts over their shoulders; others brandished boots and shirts, and one glistening brave swung a banjo at arm's-length over his flying horse's head. Another party of the despoilers discovered a shipment of silks and satins. These they dragged in bolts from the packing-cases and, tying one end of a bolt of silk to their ponies' tails, they raced, yelling, in circles around the prairie with the parti-colored silks streaming behind, the bolts bobbing and jerking along the ground like rioting garlands of a crazy May-pole dance. And, having exhausted their ingenuity and robed themselves in this wise in all manner of plunder, they set fire to the wrecked train, singing and dancing in high glee as the flames rose crackling above the trees.

Bucks, with clenched hands, watched and prayed for the arrival of the speeding relief train. The moments passed with leaden feet and the train had many miles to come. The despatcher continued his encouraging messages, but did not cease his words of caution, and, as the wreckage burned, Bucks perceived the Indians were riding in great numbers up the creek. Too late he realized what it meant. They were looking for the ford and were about to cross to his side.

CHAPTER XI

He lost no time in sending a final word to the despatcher before he started for safety, and his call was sounding when he ran back to the key.

"Stanley's train has passed Chimney Butte," said the despatcher. "Soon be with you."

Words over the wire never sounded better to the frightened boy than those words.

"The Indians are crossing the creek," Bucks answered. "Am off for the ranch."

He closed the circuit and ran out on the platform. The warriors had found the ford and the horses of the head braves were already leading a file across. Bucks threw one hurried look at them; then, summoning his strength for an endurance run, he started, with the station building between him and the enemy, for the ranch.

He had hardly got under way when, as he reached higher ground, he saw to his consternation a party of Indians in the bottom land between him and safety.

He was cut off. Hoping that he had not been seen, he threw himself flat on the ground and, turning about, crawled, behind a slight ridge that afforded concealment, stealthily back toward the station. The Indians up the creek had crossed, but were riding away from the station and toward the ranch, evidently bent on attacking it next. The flames from the burning train rose high above the creek. There seemed no place to escape to and Bucks, creeping through the sedge grass, got back to his key and called the despatcher.

"Cut off from the ranch by a second party of Indians. Will wait here for the train—where is it?"

A moment passed before the answer came. "Less than ten miles from you. Passed Driftwood Station at ten-forty."

Bucks looked at his clock. Driftwood was ten miles west. The hands stood at ten-forty-eight. Surely, he concluded, they will be here by eleven o'clock. Could he hold the station for twelve minutes? Even a show of force he knew would halt the Indians for an interval.

He hastily pushed such packages of freight as lay in the store-room up to the various windows, as slight barricades behind which he could hide to shoot, and with much effort got the largest packing-case against the platform door so they could not rush him from the creek side. For the twentieth time he looked over his revolver, placed a little store of cartridges behind each shelter, and peered again out of the windows. To his horror he perceived that the two parties had joined and were riding in a great half-circle down on the station. Evidently the Indians were coming after him before they attacked the ranch. He reported to the despatcher, and an answer came instantly. "Stanley should be within five miles. How close are they?"

"Less than half a mile."

"Have you got a gun?"

Bucks wired, "Yes."

"Can you use it?"

"Expect I'll have to."

"Shoot the minute they get within range. Never mind whether you hit anybody, bang away. What are they doing?"

Bucks ran around the room to look. "Closing in," he answered briefly.

"Can't you see the train?"

Bucks fixed his eyes upon the western horizon. He never had tried so hard in his life to see anything. Yet the sunshine reflected no sign of a friendly smoke.

"Nothing in sight," he answered; "I can't hold out much longer."

Hastily closing his key he ran to the south window. A dozen Indians, beating the alder bushes as they advanced, doubtless suspecting that he lay concealed in them, were now closest. He realized that by his very audacity in returning to the building he had gained a few precious moments. But the nearest Indians had already reached open ground, two hundred yards away, and through their short, yelping cries and their halting on the edge of the brake, he understood they were debating how he had escaped and wondering whether he had gone back into the station. He lay behind some sacks of flour watching his foes closely. Greatly to his surprise, his panic had passed and he felt collected. He realized that he was fighting for his life and meant to sell it as dearly as possible. And he had resolved to shoot the instant they started toward him.

From the table he heard the despatcher's call, but he no longer dared answer it. The Indians, with a war-whoop, urged their ponies ahead and a revolver shot rang from the station window. It was followed almost instantly by a second and a third. The Indians ducked low on their horses' necks and, wheeling, made for the willows. In the quick dash for cover one horse stumbled and threw his rider. The animal bolted and the Indian, springing to his feet, ran like a deer after his companions, but he did not escape unscathed. Two shots followed him from the station, and the Indian, falling with a bullet in his thigh, dragged himself wounded into hiding.

A chorus of cries from far and near heralded the opening of the encounter. Enraged by the repulse, a larger number of Indians riding in opened fire on the station and Bucks found himself target for a fusillade of bullets. But protected by his barricades he was only fearful of a charge, for when the Indians should start to rush the station he felt all would be over.

While he lay casting up his chances, and discharging his revolver at intervals to make a showing, the fire of the Indians slackened. This, Bucks felt, boded no good, and reckless of his store of cartridges he continued to blaze away whenever he could see a bush moving.

It was at this moment that he heard the despatcher calling him, and a message followed. "If you are alive, answer me."

Bucks ran to the key. The situation was hopeless. No train was in sight as he pressed his fingers on the button for the last time.

"Stopped their first advance and wounded one. They are going to charge——"

He heard a sharp chorus outside and, feeling what it meant, sent his last word: "Good-by." From three sides of the open ground around the building the Indians were riding down upon him. Firing as fast as he could with any accuracy, he darted from window to window, reaching the west window last. As he looked out he saw up the valley the smoke of the approaching train and understood from the fury of his enemies that they, too, had seen it. But the sight of the train now completely unnerved him. To lose his life with help a few moments away was an added bitterness, and he saw that the relief train would be too late to save him.

He fired the last cartridge in his hot revolver at the circling braves and, as he reloaded, the Indians ran up on the platform and threw themselves against the door. Fiendish faces peered through the window-panes and one Indian smashed a sash in with a war club.

Bucks realized that his reloading was useless. The cartridges were, in fact, slipping through his fingers, when, dropping his revolver, he drew Bob Scott's knife and backed up against the inner office door, just as a warrior brandishing a hatchet sprang at him.

CHAPTER XII

Before Bucks had time to think, a second Indian had sprung through the open window. A feeling of helpless rage swept over him at being cornered, defenceless; and, expecting every instant to be despatched with no more consideration than if he had been a rat, he stood at bay, determined not to be taken alive.

For an instant his mind worked clearly and with the rapidity of lightning. His life swept before him as if he were a drowning man. In that horrible moment he even heard his call clicking from the despatcher. Of the two Indians confronting him, half-naked and shining with war-paint, one appeared more ferocious than the other, and Bucks only wondered which would attack first.

He had not long to wait. The first brave raised a war club to brain him. As Bucks's straining eye followed the movement, the second Indian struck the club down. Bucks understood nothing from the action. The quick, guttural words that followed, the sharp dispute, the struggle of the first savage to evade the second and brain the white boy in spite of his antagonist—a lithe, active Indian of great strength who held the enraged warrior back—all of this, Bucks, bewildered, could understand nothing of. The utmost he could surmise was that the second warrior, from his dress and manner of authority perhaps a chief, meant to take him alive for torture. He watched the contest between the two Indians until with force and threats the chief had driven the warrior outside and turned again upon him.

It was then that Bucks, desperate, hurled himself knife in hand at the chief to engage him in final combat. The Indian, though surprised, met his onset skilfully and before Bucks could realize what had occurred he had been disarmed and tossed like a child half-way across the room.

Before he could move, the chief was standing over him. "Stop!" he exclaimed, catching Bucks's arm in a grip of steel as the latter tried to drag down his antagonist. "I am Iron Hand. Does a boy fight me?" he demanded with contempt in every word. "See your knife." He pointed to the floor. "When I was wounded by the Cheyennes you gave me venison. You have forgotten; but the Sioux is not like the white man—Iron Hand does not forget."

A fusillade of shots and a babel of yelling from outside interrupted his words. The chief paid no attention to the uproar. "Your soldiers are here. The building is on fire, but you are safe. I am Iron Hand."

So saying, and before Bucks could find his tongue, the chief strode to the rear window, with one blow of his arm smashed out the whole sash, and springing lightly through the crashing glass, disappeared.

Bucks, panting with confusion, sprang to his feet. Smoke already poured in from the freight room, and the crackling of flames and the sounds of the fighting outside reminded Bucks of Iron Hand's words. He ran to the door.

The train had pulled up within a hundred feet of the station and the railroad men in the coaches were pouring a fire upon the Indians, under the cover of which scouts were unloading, down a hastily improvised chute, their horses, together with those of such troopers as had been gathered hurriedly.

Bucks ran back into the office and opening his wooden chest threw into it what he could of his effects and tried to drag it from the burning building out upon the platform. As he struggled with the unwieldy box, two men ran up from the train toward him, staring at him as if he had been a ghost. He recognized Stanley and Dancing.

"Are you hurt?" cried Stanley hastening to his side.

"No," exclaimed Bucks, his head still swimming, "but everything will be burned."

"How in the name of God, boy, have you escaped?" demanded Stanley, as he clenched Bucks's shoulder in his hand. Dancing seized the cumbersome chest and dragged it out of danger. The Indians, jeering, as they retreated, at the railroad men, made no attempt to continue the attack, but rode away content with the destruction of the train and the station.

Stanley, assured of Bucks's safety, though he wasted no time in waiting for an explanation of it, directed the men to save what they could out of the station—it was too late to save the building—and hurried away to see to the unloading of the horses.

Bill Dancing succeeded in rescuing the telegraph instruments and with Bucks's help he got the wires rigged upon a cracker-box outside where the operator could report the story to the now desperate despatcher. The scouts and troopers were already in the saddle and, leading the way for the men, gave chase across the bottoms to the Indians.

Bob Scott, riding past Bucks reined up for a moment. "Got pretty warm for you, Bucks—eh? How did you get through?"

Bucks jumped toward him. "Bob!" he exclaimed, grasping his arm. "It was Iron Hand."

"Iron Hand!" echoed Bob, lifting his eyebrows. "Brulés, then. It will be a long chase. What did he say?"

"Why, we talked pretty fast," stammered Bucks. "He spoke about the venison but never said a blamed word about my fixing his arm."

Bob laughed as he struck his horse and galloped on to pass the news to Stanley. A detail was left to clear the cotton-woods across the creek and guard the railroad men against possible attack while clearing the wreck. The body of the unfortunate brakeman was brought across the bridge and laid in the baggage car and a tent was pitched to serve as a temporary station for Bucks.

While this was being done, Bob Scott, who had ridden farthest up the creek, appeared leading his horse and talking to a white man who was walking beside him. He had found the conductor of the wrecked train, Pat Francis, who, young though he was, had escaped the Indians long enough to reach a cave in the creek bank and whose rifle shots Bucks had heard, while Francis was holding the

Sioux at bay during the fight. The plucky conductor, who was covered with dust, was greeted with acclamations.

"He claims," volunteered Scott, speaking to Stanley, "he could have stood them off all day."

Francis's eyes fell regretfully on the dead brakeman. "If that boy had minded what I said and come with me he would have been alive now."

The wrecking train, with a gang of men from Medicine Bend, arrived late in the afternoon, and at supper-time a courier rode in from Stanley's scouting party with despatches for General Park. Stanley reported the chase futile. As Bob Scott had predicted, the Brulés had burned the ranch and craftily scattered the moment they reached the sand-hills. Instead of a single trail to follow, Stanley found fifty. Only his determination to give the Indians a punishment that they would remember held the pursuing party together, and three days afterward he fought a battle with the wily raiders, surprised in a canyon on the Frenchman River, which, though indecisive, gave Iron Hand's band a wholesome respect for the stubborn engineer.

The train service under the attacks of the Indians thus repeated, fell into serious demoralization, and an armed guard of regular soldiers rode all trains for months after the Goose Creek attack. Bucks was given a guard for his own lonely and exposed position in the person of Bob Scott, the man of all men the young operator would have wished for. And at intervals he read from his favorite novel to the scout, who still questioned whether it was a true story.

CHAPTER XIII

With Bob Scott to lead an occasional hunting trip, Bucks found the time go fast at Goose Creek and no excitement came again until later in the summer.

Where Goose Creek breaks through the sand-hills the country is flat, and, when swollen with spring rains, the stream itself has the force and fury of a mountain river. Then summer comes; the rain clouds hang no longer over the Black Hills, continuing sunshine parches the face of the great plains, and the rushing and turbulent Goose Creek ignominiously evaporates—either ascending to the skies in vapor or burrowing obscurely under the sprawling sands that lie within its course. Only stagnant pools and feeble rivulets running in widely separated channels—hiding under osiers or lurking within shady stretches of a friendly bank—remain to show where in April the noisy Goose engulfs everything within reach of its foaming wings. The creek bed becomes in midsummer a mere sandy ford that may be crossed by a child—a dry map that prints the running feet of snipe and plover, the creeping tread of the mink and the muskrat, and the slouching trail of the coyote and the wolf.

Yet there is treachery in the Goose even in its apparent repose, and the unwary emigrant sometimes comes to grief upon its treacherous bed. The sands of the Goose have swallowed up more than one heedless buffalo, and the Indian knows them too well to trust them at all.

When the railroad bridge was put across the creek, the difficulties of securing it were very considerable and Brodie, the chief engineer, was in the end forced to rely upon temporary foundations. Trainmen and engineers for months carried "slow" orders for Goose Creek bridge, and Bucks grew weary with warnings from the despatchers to careless enginemen about crossing it.

Among the worst offenders in running his engine too fast over Goose Creek bridge was Dan Baggs, who, breathing fire through his bristling red whiskers and flashing it from his watery blue eyes, feared nobody but Indians, and obeyed reluctantly everybody connected with the railroad. Moreover, he never hesitated to announce that when "they didn't like the way he ran his engine they could get somebody else to run it."

Baggs's great failing was that, while he often ran his train too fast, he wasted so much time at stations that he was always late. And it was said of him that the only instance in which he ever reached the end of his division on time was the day he ran away from Iron Hand's band of Sioux at Goose Creek—on that occasion he had made, without a doubt, a record run.

But when, one hot afternoon in August, Baggs left Medicine Bend with a light engine for Fort Park, where he was to pick up a train-load of ties, he had no thought of making further pioneer railroad history. His engine had been behaving so well that his usual charges of inefficiency against it had not for a long time been registered with the roundhouse foreman, and Dan Baggs, dreaming in the heat and sunshine of nothing worse than losing his scalp to the Indians or winning a fortune at cards—gambling was another of his failings—was pounding lightly along over the rails when he reached, without heeding it, Goose Creek bridge.

There were those who averred that after his experience with Iron Hand he always ran faster across the forbidden bridge than anywhere else. On this occasion Baggs bowled merrily along the trestle and was getting toward the middle of the river when the pony trucks jumped the rail and the drivers dropped on the ties. Dan Baggs yelled to his fireman.

It was unnecessary. Delaroo, the fireman, a quiet but prudent fellow, was already standing in the gangway prepared for an emergency. He sprang, not a minute too soon, from the engine and lighted in the sand. But Dan Baggs's fixed habit of being behind time chained him to his seat an instant too long. The bulky engine, with its tremendous impetus, shot from the trestle and plunged like a leviathan clear of the bridge and down into the wet sand of the creek-bed.

The fireman scrambled to his feet and ran forward, expecting to find his engineman hurt or killed. What was his surprise to behold Baggs, uninjured, on his feet and releasing the safety-valve of his fallen locomotive to prevent an explosion. The engine lay on its side. The crash of the breaking timbers, followed by a deafening blast of escaping steam, startled Bucks and, with Bob Scott, he ran out of the station. As he saw the spectacle in the river, he caught his breath. He lived to see other wrecks—some appalling ones—but this was his first, and the shock of seeing Dan Baggs's engine lying prone in the river, trumpeting forth a cloud of steam, instead of thundering across the bridge as he normally saw it every day, was an extraordinary one.

Filled with alarm, he ran toward the bridge expecting that the worst had happened to the engineman and fireman. But his amazement grew rather than lessened when he saw Delaroo and Baggs running for their lives toward him. He awaited them uneasily.

"What's the matter?" demanded Bucks, as Baggs, well in the lead, came within hailing distance.

"Matter!" panted Baggs, not slackening his pace. "Matter! Look at my engine! Indians!"

"Indians, your grandmother!" retorted Bob Scott mildly. "There's not an Indian within forty miles—what's the matter with you?"

"They wrecked us, Bob," declared Baggs, pointing to his roaring engine; "see for yourself, man. Them cotton-woods are full of Indians right now."

"Full of rabbits!" snorted Bob Scott. "You wrecked yourself by running too fast."

"Delaroo," demanded Dan Baggs, pointing dramatically at his taciturn fireman, who had now overtaken him, "how fast was I running?"

Peter Delaroo, an Indian half-blood himself, returned a disconcerting answer. "As fast as you could, I reckon." He understood at once that Baggs had raised a false alarm to protect himself from blame for the accident, and resented being called upon to support an absurd story.

Baggs stood his ground. "If you don't find an Indian has done this," he asserted, addressing Bob Scott with indignation, "you can have my pay check."

"Yes," returned Bob, meditatively. "I reckon an Indian did it, but you are the Indian."

"Come, stop your gabble, you boys!" blustered the doughty engineman, speaking to everybody and with a show of authority. "Bucks, notify the despatcher I'm in the river."

"Get back to your engine, then," said Scott. "Don't ask Bucks to send in a false report. And afterward," suggested Scott, "you and I, Dan, can go over and clean the Indians out of the cotton-woods."

Baggs took umbrage at the suggestion, and no amount of chaffing from Scott disconcerted him, but after Bucks reported the catastrophe to Medicine Bend the wires grew warm. Baxter was very angry. A crew was got together at Medicine Bend, and a wrecking-train made up with a gang of bridge and track men and despatched to the scene of the disaster. The operating department was so ill equipped to cope with any kind of a wreck that it was after midnight before the train got under way.

The sun had hardly risen next morning, when Bob Scott, without any words of explanation, ran into Bucks's room, woke him hurriedly, and, bidding him dress quickly, ran out. It took only a minute for Bucks to spring from his cot and get into his clothes and he hastened out of doors to learn what the excitement was about. Scott was walking fast down toward the bridge. Bucks joined him.

"What is it, Bob?" he asked hastily. "Indians?"

"Indians?" echoed Bob scornfully. "I guess not this time. I've heard of Indians stealing pretty nearly everything on earth—but not this. No Indian in this country, not even Turkey Leg, ever stole a locomotive."

"What do you mean?"

"I mean Dan Baggs's engine is gone."

Bucks's face turned blank with amazement. "Gone?" he echoed incredulously. He looked at Scott with reproach. "You are joking me."

"See if you can find it," returned Scott tersely.

As they hastened on, Bucks looked to the spot where the engine had lain the night before. It was no longer there.

He was too stunned to ask further questions. The two strode along the ties in silence. Eagerly Bucks ran to the creek bank and scanned more closely the sandy bed. It was there that the wrecked engine and tender had lain the night before. The sand showed no disturbance whatever. It was as smooth as a table. But nothing was to be seen of the engine or tender. These had disappeared as completely as if an Aladdin's slave, at his master's bidding, had picked them from their resting place and set them on top of some distant sand-hill.

"Bob," demanded Bucks, breathless, "what does it mean?"

"It means the company is out one brand-new locomotive."

"But what has happened?" asked Bucks, rubbing his eyes to make sure he was not dreaming. "Where is the engine?"

Scott pointed to the spot where the engine had lain. "It is in that quicksand," said he.

The engine, during the night, had, in fact, sunk completely into the sand. No trace was left of it or of its tender. Not a wheel or cab corner remained to explain; all had mysteriously and completely disappeared.

"Great Heavens, Bob!" exclaimed Bucks. "How will they *ever* get it out?"

"The only way they'll ever get it out, I reckon, is by keeping Dan Baggs digging there till he digs it out."

"Dan Baggs never could dig that out—how long would it take him?"

"About a hundred and seventy-five years."

As Scott spoke, the two heard footsteps behind them. Baggs and Delaroo, who had slept at the section-house, were coming down the track. "Baggs," said Scott ironically, as the sleepy-looking engineman approached, "you were right about the Indians being in the cotton-woods last night."

"I knew I was right," exclaimed Baggs, nodding rapidly and brusquely. "Next time you'll take a railroad man's word, I guess. Where are they?" he added, looking apprehensively around. "What have they done?"

"They have stolen your engine," answered Scott calmly. He pointed to the river bed. Baggs stared; then running along the bank he looked up-stream and down and came back sputtering.

"Why—what—how—what in time! Where's the engine?"

"Indians," remarked Scott sententiously, looking wisely down upon the sphinx-like quicksand. "Indians, Dan. They must have loaded the engine on their ponies during the night—did you hear anything?" he demanded, turning to Bucks. Bucks shook his head. "I thought I did," continued Scott. "Thought I heard something—what's that?"

Baggs jumped. All were ready to be startled at anything—for even Scott, in spite of his irony, had been as much astounded as any one at the first sight of the empty bed of sand. It was enough to make any one feel queerish. The noise they heard was the distant rumble of the wrecking-train.

In the east the sun was bursting over the sand-hills into a clear sky. Bucks ran to the station to report the train and the disappearance of the engine. When he had done this he ran back to the bridge. The wrecking-train had pulled up near at hand and the greater part of the men, congregated in curious groups on the bridge, were talking excitedly and watching several men down on the sand, who with spades were digging vigorously about the spot which Baggs and Delaroo indicated as the place where the engine had fallen. Others from time to time joined them, as they scraped out wells and trenches in the moist sand. These filled with water almost as rapidly as they were opened.

Urged by their foreman, a dozen additional men joined the toilers. They dug in lines and in circles, singly and in squads, broadening their field of prospecting as the laughter and jeers of their companions watching from the bridge spurred them to further toil. But not the most diligent of their efforts brought to light a single trace of the missing engine.

The wrecking crew was mystified. Many refused to believe the engine had ever fallen off the bridge. But there was the broken track! They could not escape the evidence of their eyes, even if they did scoff at the united testimony of the two men that had been on the engine when it leaped from the bridge and the two that had afterward seen it lying in the sand.

The track and bridge men without more ado set to work to repair the damage done the track and bridge. A volley of messages came from head-quarters. At noon a special car, with Colonel Stanley and the division heads arrived to investigate.

The digging was planned and directed on a larger scale and resumed with renewed vigor. Sheet piling was attempted. Every expedient was resorted to that Stanley's scientific training could suggest to bring to light the buried treasure— for an engine in those days, and so far from locomotive works, was very literally a treasure to the railroad company. Stanley himself was greatly upset. He paced the ties above where the men were digging, directing and encouraging them doggedly, but very red in the face and contemplating the situation with increasing vexation. He stuck persistently to the work till darkness set in. Meantime, the track had been opened and the wrecking-train crossed the bridge

61

and took the passing track. The moon rose full over the broad valley and the silent plains. Men still moved with lanterns under the bridge. Bucks, after a hard day's work at the key, was invited for supper to Stanley's car, where the foremen had assembled to lay new plans for the morrow. But Bob Scott, when Bucks told him, shook his head.

"They are wasting their work," he murmured. "The company is 'out.' That engine is half-way to China by this time."

It might, at least, as well have been, as far as the railroad company was concerned. The digging and sounding and scraping proved equally useless. The men dug down almost as deep as the piling that supported the bridge itself—it was in vain. In the morning the sun smiled at their efforts and again at night the moon rose mysteriously upon them, and in the distant sand-hills a thousand coyotes yelped a requiem for the lost locomotive. But no human eye ever saw so much as a bolt of the great machine again.

CHAPTER XIV

The loss of the engine at Goose Creek brought an unexpected relief to Bucks. His good work in the emergency earned for him a promotion. He was ordered to report to Medicine Bend for assignment, and within a week a new man appeared at Goose Creek to relieve him.

There was little checking up to do. Less than thirty minutes gave Bucks time to answer all of his successor's questions and pack his trunk. He might have slept till morning and taken a passenger train to Medicine Bend, but the prospect of getting away from Goose Creek at once was too tempting to dismiss. A freight train of bridge timbers pulled across the bridge just as Bucks was ready to start. Pat Francis, the doughty conductor, who, single-handed, had held Iron Hand's braves at bay, was in charge of the train. He offered Bucks a bench and blanket in the caboose for the night, and promised to have him in Medicine Bend in the morning; Bucks, nothing loath, accepted. His trunk was slung aboard and the train pulled out for Medicine Bend.

The night proved unseasonably cold. Francis built a blazing fire in the caboose stove and afterward shared his hearty supper with his guest. As the train thundered and rumbled slowly over the rough track, the conductor, while Bucks stretched out on the cushions, entertained him with stories of his experiences on the railroad frontier—not suspecting that before morning he should furnish for his listener one of the strangest of them.

Bucks curled up in his blanket late, but, in spite of unaccustomed surroundings and the pitch and lurch of the caboose, which was hardly less than the tossing of a ship in a gale, Bucks dozed while his companion and the brakeman watched. The latter, a large, heavy fellow, was a busy man, as the calls for brakes—and only hand-brakes were then known—were continual. There were no other passengers, and except for the frequent blasts of the engine whistle the night passed quietly enough.

Bucks dreamed of fighting bears with Scuffy, and found himself repeatedly rolling down precipitous mountains without landing successfully anywhere. Then he quieted into a heavy, unbroken sleep and found himself among the hills of Alleghany, hunting rabbits that were constantly changing into antelope and escaping him. Fatigued with his unceasing efforts, he woke.

A gray light, half dusk, revealed the outlines of the cab interior, as he opened his eyes, and a thundering, rumbling sound that rang in his ears and seemed everywhere about him cleared his mind and brought him back to his situation.

It was cold, and he looked at the stove. The fire was out. On the opposite side of the cab the brakeman lay on the cushions fast asleep. Outside, the thundering noises came continuously from everywhere at once. It did not occur to Bucks that the caboose was standing still. It trembled and vibrated more or less, but he noticed there was no longer any lurching and thought they had reached remarkably smooth track. They were certainly not standing still, he assured himself, as he rubbed his eyes to wake up. But perhaps they might be in the yards at Medicine Bend, with other trains rolling past them.

Somewhat confused he raised the curtain of the window near him. The sky was overcast and day was breaking. He rose higher on his elbow to look more carefully. Everywhere that his eye could reach toward the horizon the earth seemed in motion, rising and falling in great waves. Was it an earthquake? He rubbed his eyes. It seemed as if everywhere thousands of heads were tossing, and from this continual tossing and trampling came the thunder and vibration. Moreover, the caboose was not moving; of this he felt sure. Amazed, and only half-awake, he concluded that the train must have left the track and dropped into a river. The uncertainty of his vision was due, he now saw, to a storm that had swept the plains. It was blowing, with a little snow, and in the midst of the snow the mysterious waves were everywhere rising and falling.

Bucks put the curtain completely aside. The sound of his feet striking the floor aroused the conductor, who rose from his cushion with a start. "I've been asleep," he exclaimed, rubbing his eyes. "Where are we, Bucks?"

"That is what I am trying to figure out."

"Where is the brakeman?" demanded Francis. As he asked the question he saw the big fellow asleep in the corner. Francis shook him roughly. "That comes of depending on some one else," he muttered to Bucks. "I went to sleep on his promise to watch for an hour—he knew I had been up all last night and told me to take a nap. You see what happened. The moment I went to sleep, he went to sleep," exclaimed Francis in disgust. "Wake up!" he continued brusquely to the drowsy brakeman. "Where are we? What have we stopped for? What's all this noise?" Though he asked the questions fast, he expected no answer to any of them from the confused trainman and waited for none. Instead, he threw up a curtain and looked out. "Thunder and guns! Buffaloes!" he cried, and seizing his lantern ran out of the caboose door and climbed the roof-ladder. Bucks was fast upon his heels.

The freight train stood upon a wide plain and in the midst of thousands of buffaloes travelling south. As far as their eyes could reach in all directions, the astonished railroad men beheld a sea of moving buffaloes. Without further delay Francis, followed by Bucks, started along the running boards for the head end of the train.

The conductor found his train intact; but when he reached the head end he could find neither engine, tender, nor crew. All had disappeared. Running down the ladder of the head box-car, the conductor examined the draw-bar for evidence of an accident. The coupling was apparently uninjured but the tender and engine were gone. Francis, more upset than Bucks had ever seen him, or ever afterward saw him, walked moodily back to the caboose. What humiliated him more than the strange predicament in which he found himself was that he had trusted to a subordinate and gone to sleep in his caboose while on duty.

"Serves me right," he muttered, knitting his brows. "Brakeman," he added sternly, "take your lantern and flags and get out behind. The minute the buffaloes get across the track, go back two hundred yards and protect us. I will watch the head end. While these buffaloes are crossing they will be protection enough. Soon as it is daylight we will find out where we are."

The snow continued falling and the buffaloes drifted south with the storm, which was squally. Every moment, as the sky and landscape lightened, Francis, whom Bucks had followed forward, expected to see the last of the moving herd. But an hour passed and a second hour without showing any gaps in the enormous fields. And the brighter the daylight grew, the more buffaloes they could see.

Francis stormed at the situation, but he could do nothing. Finally, and as hope was deserting him, he heard the distant tooting of an engine whistle. It grew louder and louder until Bucks could hear the ringing of a bell and the hissing of the open cylinder cocks of a slow-moving locomotive. Gaps could now be discerned in the great herds of buffaloes, and through the blowing snow the uncertain outlines of the backing engine could dimly be seen. Francis angrily watched the approaching engine, and, as soon as it had cleared the last of the stumbling buffaloes on the track, he walked forward to meet it and greeted the engineman roughly.

"What do you mean by setting my train out here on the main track in the middle of the night?" he demanded ferociously, and those that knew Pat Francis never wanted to add to his anger when it was aroused.

"Don't get excited," returned Dan Baggs calmly, for it was the redoubtable Baggs who held the throttle. "I found I was getting short of water. We are just coming to Blackwood Hill and I knew I could never make Blackwood Siding with the train. So I uncoupled and ran to the Blackwood tank for water. We are all right now. Couple us up. If I hadn't got water, we should have been hung up here till we got another engine."

"Even so," retorted Francis, "you needn't have been all night about it."

"But when we started back there were about ten million buffaloes on the track. If I had been heading into them with the cow-catcher I shouldn't have been

64

afraid. But I had to back into them, and if I had crippled one it would have upset the tender."

"Back her up," commanded Francis curtly, "and pull us out of here."

Meantime there was much excitement at the despatchers' office in Medicine Bend over the lost train. It had been reported out of White Horse Station on time, and had not reported at Blackwood. For hours the despatcher waited vainly for some word from the bridge timbers. When the train reported at Blackwood Station, the message of Francis explaining the cause of the tie-up seemed like a voice from the tombs. But the strain was relieved and the train made fast time from Blackwood in. About nine o'clock in the morning it whistled for the Medicine Bend yards and a few moments later Bucks ran upstairs in the station building to report for assignment.

CHAPTER XV

He found Baxter needing a man in the office, and Bucks was asked to substitute until Collins, the despatcher who was ill, could take his trick again. This brought Bucks where he was glad to be, directly under Stanley's eye, but it brought also new responsibilities, and opened his mind to the difficulties of operating a new and already over-taxed line in the far West, where reliable men and available equipment were constantly at a premium.

The problem of getting and keeping good men was the hardest that confronted the operating department, and the demoralization of the railroad men from the life in Medicine Bend grew steadily worse as the new town attracted additional parasites. When Bucks, after his return, took his first walk after supper up Front Street, he was not surprised at this. Medicine Bend was more than ten times as noisy, and if it were possible to add any vice to its viciousness this, too, it would seem, had been done.

As was his custom, he walked to the extreme end of Front Street and turning started back for the station, when he encountered Baxter, the chief despatcher. Baxter saw Bucks first and spoke.

"I thought you were taking your sleep at this time," returned Bucks, greeting him.

"So I should be," he replied, "but we are in trouble. Dan Baggs is to take out the passenger train to-night, and no one can find him. He is somewhere up here in one of these dives and has forgotten all about his engine. It is enough to set a man crazy to have to run trains with such cattle. Bucks, suppose you take one side of the street while I take the other, and help me hunt him up."

"What shall we do?"

"Look in every door all the way down-street till we find him. If we don't get the fellow on his engine, there will be no train out till midnight. Say nothing to anybody and answer no questions; just find him."

Baxter started down the right-hand side of the long street and Bucks took the left-hand side. It was queer business for Bucks, and the sights that met him at every turn were enough to startle one stouter than he. He controlled his disgust and ignored the questions sometimes hurled at him by drunken men and women, intent only on getting his eye on the irresponsible Baggs.

Half-way down toward the square he reached a dance hall. The doors were spread wide open and from within came a din of bad music, singing, and noise of every kind.

Bucks entered the place with some trepidation. In the rear of the large room was a raised platform extending the entire width of it. At one end of the platform stood a piano which a man pounded incessantly and fiercely. Other performers were singing and dancing to entertain a motley and disorderly audience seated in a still more disorderly array before them.

At the right of the room a long bar stretched from the street back as far as the stage, and standing in front of this, boisterous groups of men were smoking and drinking, or wrangling in tipsy fashion. The opposite side of the big room was given over to gambling devices of every sort, and this space was filled with men sitting about small tables and others sitting and standing along one side of long tables, at each of which one man was dealing cards, singly, out of a metal case held in his hand. Other men clustered about revolving wheels where, oblivious of everything going on around them, they watched with feverish anxiety a ball thrown periodically into the disc by the man operating the wheel.

Bucks walked slowly down the room the full length of the bar, scanning each group of men as he passed. He crossed the room behind the chairs where the audience of the singers and dancers sat. He noticed, when he reached this, the difference in the faces he was scrutinizing. At the gambling tables the men saw and heard nothing of what went on about them. He walked patiently on his quest from group to group, unobserved by those about him, but without catching a sight of the elusive engineman. As he reached the end of the gambling-room, he hesitated for a moment and had finished his quest when, drawn by curiosity, he stopped for an instant to watch the scene about the roulette wheels.

Almost instantly he heard a sharp voice behind him. "What are you doing here?"

Bucks, surprised, turned to find himself confronted by the black-bearded passenger conductor, David Hawk. Baxter's admonition to say nothing of what he was doing confused Bucks for an instant, and he stammered some evasive answer.

Hawk, blunt and stern in word and manner, followed the evasion up sharply: "Don't you know this is no place for you?" and before Bucks could answer, Hawk had fixed him with his piercing eyes.

"You want to hang around a gambling-table, do you? You want to watch how it is done and try it yourself sometime? You want to see how much smarter you can play the game than these sheep-heads you are watching?

"Don't talk to me," he exclaimed sternly as Bucks tried to explain. "I've seen boys in these places before. I know where they end. If I ever catch you in a gambling-den again I'll throw you neck and heels into the river."

The words fell upon Bucks like a cloud-burst. Before he could return a word or catch his breath Hawk strode away.

As Bucks stood collecting his wits, Baggs, the man for whom he was looking, passed directly before his eyes. Bucks sprang forward, caught Baggs by the arm, and led him toward the door, as he gave him Baxter's message. Baggs, listening somewhat sheepishly, made no objection to going down to take his train and walked through the front door with Bucks out into the street.

As they did this, a red-faced man who was standing on the doorstep seized Bucks's sleeve and attempted to jerk him across the sidewalk. Bucks shook himself free and turned on his assailant. He needed no introduction to the hard cheeks, one of which was split by a deep scar. It was Perry, Rebstock's crony, whom Stanley had driven out of Sellersville on the Spider Water.

"What are you doing around here interfering with my business?" he demanded of Bucks harshly. "I've watched you spying around. The next time I catch you trying to pull a customer out of my place, I'll knock your head off."

Bucks eyed the bully with gathering wrath. He was already upset mentally, and taken so suddenly and unawares lost his temper and his caution. "If you do, it will be the last head you knock off in Medicine Bend," he retorted. "When I find trainmen in your joint that are needed on their runs, I'll pull them out every time. The safest thing you can do is to keep quiet. If the railroad men ever get started after you, you red-faced bully, they'll run you and your whole tribe into the river again."

It was a foolish defiance and might have cost him his life, though Bucks knew he was well within the truth in what he said. Among the railroad men the feeling against the gamblers was constantly growing in bitterness. Perry instantly attempted to draw a revolver, when a man who had been watching the scene unobserved stepped close enough between him and Bucks to catch Perry's eye. It was Dave Hawk again. What he had just heard had explained things to him and he stood now grimly laughing at the enraged gambler.

"Good for the boy," he exclaimed. "Want to get strung up, do you, Perry? Fire that gun just once and the vigilantes will have a rope around your neck in five minutes."

Perry, though furious, realized the truth of what Hawk said. He poured a torrent of abuse upon Bucks, but made no further effort to use his gun. The dreaded word "vigilantes" had struck terror to the heart of a man who had once been in their hands and escaped only by an accident.

"You know what he said is so, don't you?" laughed Hawk savagely. "What? You don't?" he demanded, as Perry tried to face him down. "You'll be lucky, when that time comes, if you don't get your heels tangled up with a telegraph pole before you reach the river," concluded Hawk tauntingly.

"Let him keep away from me if he doesn't want trouble," snarled the discomfited gambler, eying Bucks threateningly. But he was plainly out-faced, and retreated, grumbling, toward the dance-hall steps.

Dan Baggs, at the first sign of hostilities, had fled. Bucks, afraid of losing him, now followed, leaving Hawk still abusing the gambler, but when he overtook the engineman he found he was going, as he had promised, straight to the roundhouse.

It was almost time for the night trick. Bucks hastened upstairs to the despatchers' office and reported to Baxter, who had returned ahead of him and was elated at Bucks's success. Before the young substitute took up his train-sheet, he told the chief despatcher of how strangely the conductor, Dave Hawk, had talked to him.

"He has a reason for it," responded Baxter briefly.

"What reason?"

"There is as good a railroad man as ever lived," said Baxter, referring to the black-bearded conductor. "He is the master of us all in the handling of trains. He could be anything anybody is on this line to-day that he might want to be but for one thing. If he hadn't ruined his own life, Dave Hawk could be superintendent here. He knows whereof he speaks, Bucks."

"What do you mean?"

"I mean he is a gambler. Did you hear the shooting after I left you?"

"No, what was it?"

"It must have been while you were in Perry's. Not five minutes after we parted, a saloon-keeper shot a woman down right in front of me; I was standing less than ten feet from her when she fell," said the despatcher, recounting the incident. "But I was too late to protect her; and I should probably have been shot myself if I had tried to."

"Was the brute arrested?"

"Arrested! Who arrests anybody in this town?"

"How long is this sort of thing going on?" asked Bucks, sitting down and signing a transfer.

"How long!" echoed the despatcher, taking up his hat to go to his room. "I don't know how long. But when their time comes—God help that crowd up Front Street!"

CHAPTER XVI

Following Collins's return to duty, Bucks was assigned to a new western station, Point of Rocks. It was in the mountains and where Casement, now laying five and even six miles of track a day, had just turned over a hundred and eighty miles to the operating department. Bucks, the first operator ever sent to the lonely place afterward famous in railroad story, put his trunk aboard a freight train the next morning and started for his destination.

The ride through the mountains was an inspiration. A party of army officers and their wives, preferring to take the day run for the scenery, were bound for one of the mountain posts, Fort Bridger, and they helped to make the long day journey in the cabin car, with its frequent stops and its laborious engine-puffing over the mountain grades, a pleasant one. The women made coffee on a cabin stove and Bucks, the only other passenger, was invited to lunch with them.

When the train stopped at Point of Rocks and Bucks got off, the sun was setting, and though the thin, clear air brought the distant mountains very close, the prospect was not a cheerful one. In every direction mountain ranges, some brown and others snow-capped, rose upon the horizon. Where the railroad line made a tortuous way among the barren buttes that dotted the uneven plain all about, there was not a spear of grass nor a living thing except the stunted sage-brush of the alkali plain. In the midst of this desert a great upheaval of granite rock thrown squarely across the direct path of the railroad opposed its straight course and made a long reverse curve necessary. This was Point of Rocks.

"You," said Stanley once to Bucks, "may live to see this railroad built across these mountains as it should be built. There will be no sharp curves then, no heavy grades such as these our little engines have to climb now. Great compound locomotives will pull trains of a hundred cars up grades of less than one per cent and around two and three degree curves. These high wooden bridges will all be replaced by big rock and earth fills. Tunnels will pierce the heights that cannot be scaled by easy grades, and electric power supplied by these mountain streams themselves will take the place of steam made by coal and hauled hundreds of miles to give us costly motive power. You may live, Bucks, to see all of this; I shall not. When it comes, think of me."

But there was no thought now in Bucks's mind of what the future might bring to that forbidding desert. He saw only a rude station building, just put up, and as the train disappeared, he dragged into this his trunk and hand-bag, and in that act a new outpost of civilization was established in the great West.

He called up Medicine Bend, reported, lighted a fire in the little stove, and the spot in the desert known now to men as Point of Rocks for the first time in the story of the world became a part of it—was linked to the world itself.

But the place was lonely beyond words, and Bucks had a hard time to keep it from being too much so for him. He walked at different times over the country in every direction, and one night after a crudely prepared supper he strolled out on the platform, desperate for something to do. Desolation marked the landscape everywhere. He wandered aimlessly across the track and seeing nothing better to interest him began climbing Point of Rocks.

The higher he climbed the more absorbed he became. Youth and strength lent ardor to the ascent, and Bucks, soon forgetting everything below, was scaling the granite pile that towered above him. For thirty minutes, without a halt, he continued to climb, and reaching after a while what seemed the highest ledge of the rocky spur, he walked out upon it to the very edge and was rewarded for his labor with a magnificent panorama of the mountain divide.

In the west the sky was still golden and, though clouds appeared to be banking heavily in the north, the view of the distant peaks was unobstructed. From where he sat he could almost have thrown a stone into one tiny mountain stream that cut a silver path toward the setting sun, and another, a hundred yards away, that flowed gently toward the rising sun. And he knew—for Bill Dancing had told him—that the one rill emptied at last into the Pacific Ocean, and the other into the Atlantic Ocean. Alongside these tiny streams he could plainly trace the overland trail of the emigrant wagons, and, cutting in straighter lines, but following the same general direction, lay the right-of-way of the new transcontinental railroad.

Beyond, in every direction, stretched great plateaus, and above these rugged mountain chains, lying in what seemed the eternal solitude of the vast desert. He was alone with the sunset, and stood for some moments silenced by the scene before him. When a sound did at length reach his ear as he sat spellbound, it brought him back to himself with the suddenness of a shock.

At first he heard only distant echoes of a short, muffled blow, irregularly repeated and seeming familiar to the ear. As he speculated upon what the sound might be, it grew gradually plainer and came seemingly nearer. He bent his eyes down the valley to the west and scanned the wagon-trail and the railroad track as far as he could in the dusk, but could see nothing. Then the muffle of the sound was at once lifted. It came from the other direction, and, turning his eyes, he saw emerging from a small canyon that hid the trail to the east, a covered emigrant wagon, drawn by a large team of horses and driven by a man sitting in front of the hood, making its way slowly up the road toward the station.

The heavy play of the wheel-hubs on the axles echoed now very plainly upon his ears, and he sat watching the outfit and wondering whether the travellers would camp for the night near him and give him what he craved most of all, a little human society. The horses passed the station, and as they did so, the driver peered intently at the new building, looking back around the side of the canvas cover, and straining his neck to see all he could see, while the horses moved along.

This would have seemed to Bucks mere idle curiosity had he not noticed that some one within the wagon parted the canvas flaps at the rear as it went by and likewise inspected the building with close attention. Even this was no especial incident for wonderment, nor was Bucks surprised when the emigrants, after pursuing their way until they were well out of sight of the station itself, guided their wagon from the trail into a little depression along the creek as if to make camp for the night. The driver, a tall, thin man, wearing a slouch hat, got down from the front of the wagon and walked with a shambling gait to the head of his horses and loosened their bridles. While the horses were drinking, a second man, carrying a rifle, climbed down from the rear of the wagon. He was of a shorter and stockier build, and on one side the brim of his soft hat had been torn away so that it hung loosely over one ear, the other ear being covered only by a shock of dusty hair.

A third man emerged from under the canvas cover, dropping down almost behind the second—a fat man who looked about him with suspicion as he slowly drew a rifle out of the wagon. The driver joined his companions for a brief conference, and when it was finished the three men, examining their rifles, walked back up the road toward the station. As they neared it, two of them loitered back and presently took their places behind convenient rocks where, without being seen, they could see everything. The third man, the driver, carrying his rifle on his arm, walked ahead, crossed the road, and, proceeding with some care, stepped up on the platform and pushed open the door of the station building.

Bucks, perched high on the rocky spur above the scene, looked on, not knowing just what to make of it all. As he saw the two men conceal themselves, he wondered what sort of a call the third man intended making on the new agent, and why he should leave two armed men close at hand in ambush when calling on one lone telegraph operator. Bucks began to feel a bit creepy and watched the scene unfolding below with keen attention. The driver of the wagon getting no response as he opened the door, walked inside, and for a moment was not seen. He soon reappeared, and, stepping to the side of the building signalled his companions to come up. Bucks saw them emerge from their hiding-places and join the driver at the station door.

A second conference followed. It was briefer than the first, but there seemed some difference of opinion among the three men, and the talk terminated abruptly by the driver's clubbing his rifle and deliberately smashing in the sash of the window before which he was standing.

Whatever had held Bucks spellbound thus far released him suddenly for action when he saw the rifle-stock raised and heard the crash of the glass. He jumped up, and running to the edge of the ledge nearest the station yelled at the marauder and shook his finger at him vigorously. The attack on his habitation was too much for Bucks's composure, and, although he knew his words could not be heard from where he stood, he felt he could frighten the intruders.

This was his second mistake. No sooner had his visitors sighted him than two guns were turned on him and instantly fired. He jumped back before the fat man, who, slower than his companions, had some difficulty in shooting so high above his head, could get his gun up. Afterward, Bucks learned how providential this was, inasmuch as the big fellow was the deadliest shot of the three.

But at the moment, danger was the last thing the operator thought of. The unprovoked and murderous attack infuriated him, and again forgetting his caution he drew his own revolver without hesitation, and, running to a more protected spot, leaned over the ledge and fired point-blank into the group, as they looked up to see what had become of him.

71

If it had been his intention to hit any one of them with his bullets, his shooting was a failure and some experience in after years among men practised in gunnery convinced him that to aim at three men is not the right way to hit one.

But if he had meant only to create a sensation his move was successful beyond his greatest expectation. Had a bomb been exploded on the platform the marauders could not have scattered more quickly. Bucks never in his life had seen three men move so fast. The fat man, indeed, had given Bucks the impression of being heavy and slow in his movements. He now made a surprising exhibition of agility, and Bucks to his astonishment, saw him distancing his leaner companions and sprinting for the shelter at a pace that would have made a jack-rabbit take notice.

Bucks, somewhat keyed up, fired twice again at the fleeing men, but with no more effect than to kick up the dust once behind and once ahead of them as they ran. The instant they reached the rocks where they found shelter Bucks drew back out of sight, and none too soon, for as he pulled himself away from the ledge, a rifle cracked viciously from below and the slug threw a chunk of granite almost up into his face; the fat man was evidently having his innings.

Bucks, out of immediate danger, lay perfectly still for a few moments casting up the strange situation he found himself in. Why the men should have acted as they had, was all a mystery, but thieves or outlaws they evidently were, and outlaws in this country he already well knew were men who would stop at nothing.

He realized, likewise, that he was in grave danger. The night was before him. No train would be through before morning. He could not reach his key by which he might have summoned aid instantly. For a moment he lay thinking. Then taking off his hat he stuck his head carefully forward; it was greeted at once by a bullet. The lesson was obvious and next time he wanted to reconnoitre he stuck his hat forward first on the muzzle of his gun, as he had often read of frontiersmen doing, and, having drawn a shot, stuck his head out afterward for a quick look. All that remained in the open was the team and wagon, but this left the outlaws at a disadvantage, for if they wanted to get their outfit and go on their way they must expose themselves to Bucks's fire. While they might feel that one operator, armed with a revolver he hardly knew how to use, was not a dangerous foe, a Colt's, even in the hands of a boy who had thus far fired first and aimed afterward, was not wholly to be despised. An accident might happen even under such conditions, and the three men, knowing that darkness would soon leave them free, waited in absolute silence.

Night fell very soon and the light of the stars, though leaving objects visible upon the high ledge, left the earth in impenetrable darkness. Strain his eyes as he would, Bucks could perceive nothing below. He could hear, however, and one of the first sounds audible was that of the wagon moving quietly away. It was a welcome sound, even though he dared not hope his troublesome visitors would withdraw without further mischief. His chief concern at this juncture was to get safely, if he could, down the rocks and into the station to give the alarm to the despatcher; for he made no doubt that the outlaws, on their wagon trip west, would damage in any way they might be able railroad supplies and property along their way.

Before Bucks had climbed down very far and after he had made one or two startling missteps, he began to consider that it was one thing to get up a rough arête in daylight and quite another to get down one in the darkness. The heavy clouds moving down from the north had massed above Point of Rocks, and he heard once in a while an ominous roll of thunder, as he slipped and slid along and bruised his hands and feet upon the rocks.

He had with great care got about half-way down, when the pitch darkness below him was pierced by a small flame which he took at first for the blaze of a camp fire. In another moment he was undeceived. The station was on fire. It was evidently the last effort of the outlaws to wreak vengeance as they left. Bucks clambered over the rocks in great alarm. He thought he might reach the building in time to save it, and, forgetting the danger of being shot should his enemies remain lying in wait, he made his way rapidly down the Point. The flames now burst from the east window of the station, and he despaired of saving it, but he hurried on until he heard the crack of a rifle, felt his cap snatched from his head and fell backward against the face of the rock. As he lost consciousness he slipped and rolled headlong down the steep ledge.

CHAPTER XVII

How long Bucks lay in the darkness he did not know, but he woke to consciousness with thunder crashing in his ears and a flood of rain beating on his upturned face. When he opened his eyes he was blinded by sheets of lightning trembling across the sky, and he turned his face from the pelting rain until he could collect himself.

While he lay insensible from the shock of the bullet, which providentially had only grazed his scalp, the storm had burst over the mountains drowning everything before it. Water fell in torrents, and the desert below him was one wide river. Water danced and swam down the rocks and ran in broad, shallow waves over the sand, and the scene was light as day. Thunder peals crashed one upon another like salvoes of artillery, deafening and alarming the confused boy, and the rain poured without ceasing. Continuing waves of lightning revealed the railroad and station building before him and he realized that he had fallen the rest of the way down from where he had been fired at on the face of the Point.

He took quick stock of his condition and, rising to his feet, found himself only sore and bruised. He pressed his way through the flood to the track, gained the platform, and, judging rightly that his assailants had abandoned their fight, entered the half-burned building unafraid. Rain poured in one corner where the roof had burned away before the storm had put out the fire.

Stumbling through the débris that covered the floor, Bucks made his way to the operator's table and put his hand up to cut in the lightning arrester. He was too late. The fire had taken everything ahead of him, and his hope of getting into communication with the despatchers was next dashed by the discovery that his instruments were wrecked.

He sat down—his chair was intact—much disheartened. But without delay he opened the drawer of the table and feeling for his box of cartridges found that the thieves had overlooked it. This he slipped into his pocket with a feeling of relief, and, as he sat, rain-soaked and with the water dripping from his hair, he reloaded his revolver and made such preparations as he could to barricade the inner door and wait for the passing of the storm.

From time to time, awed by the fury of the elements, he looked into the night. It seemed as if the valley as far as he could see was a vast lake that rippled and danced over the rocks. Bucks had never conceived of a thunderstorm like this. Until it abated there was nothing he could do, and he sat in wretched discomfort, hour after hour, waiting for the night to pass and listening to the mighty roar of the waters as they swept broadside down the divide carrying everything ahead of them. Before daylight the violence of the storm wore itself away, but the creek in the little canyon south of the right-of-way, dashing its swollen bulk against the granite walls, pounded and roared with the fury of a cataract.

When day broke, ragged masses of gray cloud scudded low across the sky. The rain had ceased, and in the operator's room Bucks, aided by the first rays of daylight, was struggling to get the telegraph wires disentangled to send a message. His hopes, as the light increased and he saw the ruin caused by the fire, were very slender, but he kept busily at the wreckage and getting, at length, two severed strands of the wires to show a current, began sending his call, followed by a message for help to Medicine Bend. He worked at this for thirty minutes unceasingly, then, looking around on every side of the building, he satisfied himself that he was alone and, dropping down at his table, leaned upon it with his elbows, and, tired, wet, and begrimed, fell fast asleep.

He was roused by the distant whistle of a locomotive. Opening his eyes, he saw the sun streaming through the east side of the building where the window casement had burned away. Shaking off the heaviness of his slumber he hastened out to see an engine and box-car coming from the east. From the open door of the car men were waving their hats. Bucks answered by swinging his arm.

The engine stopped before the station and Bob Scott, followed by Dancing, Dave Hawk, and the train crew sprang from the caboose steps and surrounded him. They had brought two horses and Bucks saw that all the men were armed. It took only a minute to tell the story, and the party scattered to view the destruction and look for clues to the perpetrators.

Scott and Dancing were especially keen in their search, but they found nothing to suggest who the vandals were. They listened again to Bucks, as he repeated his story with more detail, and held a hurried conference in which Dave Hawk took charge. Meantime the men were tearing up planks from the platform to make a chute for unloading the horses.

Bucks's excitement increased as he saw the businesslike preparations for the chase. "Have you any idea you can catch them, Bob?" he asked feverishly.

Bob Scott's smile was not a complete answer. "How can you catch anybody in *this* country?" continued Bucks, regarding the scout sceptically. But Scott looked across the interminable waste of sage-brush and rock as if he felt at home with it.

"If they stick to the wagon," he explained leisurely, "we will have them in an hour or two, Bucks. A man might as well travel around here with a brass band as to try to get away with a wagon track behind him. If they stick to the wagon, we are bound to have them in two or three hours at most. You are sure they didn't have a led horse?"

"They had nothing but the team," said Bucks.

"In that case if they give up the wagon, three of them will have to ride two horses. They can't go fast in that way. We will get some of them, Bucks, sure— somehow, sometime, somewhere. We have got to get them. How could I hold my job if I didn't get them?"

That which had seemed impossible to Bucks looked more hopeful after Bob had smiled again. Dancing was busy installing the new telegraph outfit. While this was going on, Scott saddled the horses and, when he and Dave Hawk had mounted, the two rode rapidly down the emigrant trail toward Bitter Creek. The train was held until Dancing could get the instruments working again; then, at Hawk's request, it was sent down the Bitter Creek grade after himself and Scott; the trail followed the railroad for miles. Dancing remained with Bucks to guard against further attack.

The two railroad men rode carefully along the heavy ruts of the emigrant trail, from which all recent tracks had been obliterated by the flood, knowing that they would strike no sign of the wagon until it had been started after the storm. They had covered in this manner less than two miles when, rounding a little bend, they saw a covered emigrant wagon standing in the road not half a mile from the railroad track.

Scott led quickly toward concealment and from behind a shoulder of rock to which the two rode they could see that the wagon had been halted and the horses, strangely entangled in the harness, were lying in front of it. Scott and Hawk dismounted and, crawling up the shoulder where they could see without being seen, waited impatiently for some sign of life from the suspicious outfit. The description Bucks had given fitted the wagon very well, and the two lay for a time waiting for something to happen, and exchanging speculations as to what the situation might mean. They were hoping that the thieves might, if they had gone away, return, and with this thought restrained their impatience.

"It may be a trick to get us up to shooting distance, Bob," suggested Hawk when Scott proposed they should close in.

"But that wouldn't explain why the horses are lying there in that way, Dave. Something else has happened. Those horses are dead; they haven't moved. Suppose I circle the outfit," suggested Scott benevolently.

"Take care they don't get a shot at you."

"If they can get a shot at me before I can at them they are welcome," returned Scott as he picked up his bridle rein. "From what Bucks told me I don't think a great deal of their shooting. He is a level-headed boy, that long-legged operator." And Scott, with some quiet grimaces, recounted Bucks's story of his descent of Point of Rocks the night before, under the fire of the three desperadoes.

That he himself was now taking his own life in his hands as he started on a perilous reconnoissance, cost him no thought. Such a situation he was quite used to. But for a green boy from the East to put up so unequal a fight seemed to the experienced scout a most humorous proceeding.

He mounted his horse and directing Hawk what to do if he should be hit, set out to ride completely around the suspected wagon. The canvas cover was the uncertain element in the situation. It might conceal nobody, and yet it might conceal three rifles waiting for an indiscreet pursuer to come within range. Scott, taking advantage of the uneven country, rode circumspectly to the south, keeping the object of his caution well in view, and at times, under cover of friendly rocks, getting up quite close to it.

Before he had completed half his ride he had satisfied himself as to the actual state of affairs. Yet his habitual caution led him to follow out his original purpose quite as carefully as if he had reached no conclusion. When he crossed the trail west of the wagon, he looked closely for fresh tracks, but there were none. He then circled to the north and was soon able, by dismounting, to crawl under cover within a hundred yards of the heads of the horses. When he got up to where he could see without being seen he perceived clearly that his surmise had been correct.

Both horses lay dead in the harness. From the front seat of the wagon a boot protruded; nothing more could be seen. Scott now, by signals, summoned Dave Hawk from where he lay, and when the swarthy conductor reached the scout, Scott called out loudly at the wagon.

There was no answer, no movement, no sound. Things began to seem queer; in the bright blaze of sunshine, and with the parched desert glistening after the welcome rain, there in the midst of the vast amphitheatre of mountains lay the dead horses before the mysterious wagon. But nowhere about was any sign of life, and the wagon might hold within its white walls death for whoever should unwarily approach it.

Bob Scott had no idea, however, of sacrificing himself to any scheme that might have occurred to the enemy to lure him within danger. He called out again at the top of his voice and demanded a surrender. No sound gave any response, and raising his rifle he sent a bullet through the extreme top of the canvas cover midway back from the driver's seat.

The echoes of the report crashed back to the rocks, but brought nothing from the silence of the emigrant wagon. A second shot followed, tearing through the side board of the wagon-box itself; yet there was no answer. Scott, taking his horse, while Hawk remained in hiding and covered the scene with his own rifle,

76

led the horse so that it served as a shelter and walked directly toward the wagon itself. As he neared it he approached from the front, pausing at times to survey what he saw. Hawk watched him lead his unwilling horse, trembling with fear, up to the dead team as they lay in the bright sunlight, and saw Scott take hold of the protruding boot, peer above it into the wagon itself and, without turning his head, beckon Hawk to come up.

Under the canvas, the driver of the wagon lay dead with the lines clutched in his stiffened fingers, just as he had fallen when death struck his horses. The two frontiersmen needed no explanation of what they saw in the scarred and blackened face of the outlaw. A bolt of lightning had killed him and stricken both horses in the same instant. Bob crawled into the wagon and with Hawk's help dragged the dead man forward into the sunlight. Both recognized him. It was Bucks's assailant and enemy, the Medicine Bend and Spider Water gambler, Perry.

CHAPTER XVIII

The two men, aided by the crew of the train that now came down the Bitter Creek grade, got the dead body of the outlaw back to Point of Rocks just as a mixed train from the east reached there, with Stanley and a detail of cavalry aboard. Stanley walked straight to Bucks, caught him by the shoulders, and shook him as if to make sure he was all right.

"Gave you a warm reception, did they, Bucks?"

"Moderately warm, colonel."

Stanley shook his head. "It is all wrong. They never should have sent you out here alone," he declared brusquely. "These superintendents seem to think they are railroading in Ohio instead of the Rocky Mountains. Dave," he continued, turning to Hawk as the latter came up, "I hear you have just brought in Perry dead. What have we got here, anyway?"

"Some of the Medicine Bend gang," returned Hawk tersely.

"What are they doing?"

"Evening up old scores, I guess."

Stanley looked at the dead man as they laid him out on the platform: "And hastening their own day of reckoning," he said. "There shall be no more of this if we have to drive every man of the gang out of the country. Who do you think was with Perry, Bob?" he demanded, questioning Scott.

"There is nothing to show that till we get them—and we ought to be after them now," returned the scout. "But," he added softly as he hitched his trousers, "I think one of the two might be young John Rebstock."

"You need lose no time, Bob. Here are ten men with fresh horses at your orders." Stanley pointed to the troopers who were unloading their mounts.

"Give Dave and me three of the best of these men," said Scott. "I will follow the west trail. Put a sergeant with the others on the trail east to make sure they haven't doubled back on us—but I don't think they have."

"Why?"

"They must have stolen that team and wagon, that is certain. More than likely they murdered the man they took it from. The trail is probably alive with men looking for them. These fellows were trying to get to Casement's camp for gambling, and probably they are heading that way fast now. We will pick those fellows up, colonel, somewhere between here and Bridger's Gap."

The three troopers that Scott selected were told off and, after a few rapid arrangements for sending back information, the five men of the west-trail party, headed by Scott and Dave Hawk, rode down Bitter Creek and, scattering in a wide skirmish line wherever the formation of the country permitted, scanned the ground for signs of the fugitives.

"We shan't find anything till we get to where they were when the rain stopped," Scott told the trooper near whom he was riding. It was, in fact, nearly ten miles from Point of Rocks before they picked up the footprints of two men travelling apart from each other, but headed north and west. These they followed on a long détour away from the regular wagon road until the two trails turned and entered, from the southwest, a camp made the night before by a big trading outfit on the regular overland trail.

Here, of course, all trace of the men disappeared. It was now drawing toward evening. Scott resolved to follow the trading outfit, but the party still rode slowly to make sure the men they wanted did not sneak away from the wagons of their new-found friends. The pursuers rode steadily on, and as the sun went down they perceived in a small canyon ahead of them the wagons of the outfit they were trailing, parked in a camp for the night.

Scott gave the troopers directions as to where to post themselves, at some distance east and west of the canyon, to provide against a sortie of the fugitives and, riding with Hawk directly into the camp, asked for the boss. He appeared after some delay and proved to be a French trader with supplies for Salt Lake.

Hawk, whose long visage and keen eyes gave him a particularly stern air— and David Hawk was never very communicative or very warm-mannered— asked the questions. The Frenchman was civil, but denied having any men with him except those he had brought from the Missouri River. However, he offered to line up his men for the railroad party to look over. To this Hawk agreed, and, when the word had been passed, the entire force of the trader were assembled in front of the head wagon.

Scott rode slowly up the line scrutinizing each face, and, turning again, rode down the line. Once he stopped and questioned a suspicious-looking teamster wearing a hat that answered Bucks's description, but the man's answers were satisfactory.

When Scott had finished his inspection the men started to disband. Hawk stopped them. "Stay where you are," he called out curtly. Turning to the Frenchman, he added: "We will have to search your wagons."

Again the trader made no objection, though some of his men did.

The three troopers were signalled in, and posted so there could be no dodging from one wagon to another, and Hawk gave them orders, loud enough for all to hear, to shoot on sight any one leaving the wagons. And while he himself kept command of the whole situation, Scott dismounted and accompanied by the trader began the search. The hunt was tedious and the teamsters murmured at the delay to their camp work. But the search went forward unrelentingly. Not a corner capable of concealing a dog was overlooked by the painstaking Indian and not until he had reached the last wagon was his hope exhausted.

This wagon stood at the extreme end of a wash-out in the side of the canyon itself. It was filled with bales of coarse red blankets, but no man was to be found among them.

Scott did find something, however, in a sort of a nest fashioned among the bales near the middle of the wagon. What would have escaped an eye less trained to look for trifles attracted his at once. It was a dingy metal tag. Scott picked it up. It bore the name of a Medicine Bend saloon and the heads of three horses, from the design of which the saloon itself took a widely known and ill name. He laid his hand on the blanket from which he had picked the tag. The wool was still warm.

Scott only smiled to himself. Both ends of the little canyon were guarded. From where he was searching the scout peered carefully out at the canyon walls. There were hiding-places, but they were hardly large enough to conceal a man. It was somewhere in the rocks close at hand that the fugitives had found a temporary refuge; but they could not now escape—nor could they be far from the wagon.

Without losing sight of the surroundings, Scott, disclosing nothing of his discovery to the trader, announced that he was satisfied and that the men he wanted did not appear to be there. He added, however, that if the Frenchman had no objection his party would pitch camp close by and ride with him in the morning. The Frenchman maintained his courtesy by inviting the party to take supper with him, and Scott, agreeing to return, rode away with Hawk and the three troopers.

They had not ridden far, when Bob dismounted the party and leaving the horses with one trooper set two as pickets and posted himself in hiding on one side the canyon, with Hawk on the other, to watch the camp. What he saw or whether his patience was in any degree rewarded no one could have told from his inscrutable face as he walked into the camp at dusk and sat down with the trader to supper. The moon was just rising and down at the creek, a little way from where Scott sat, some belated teamsters were washing their hands and faces and preparing their own supper. Scott ate slowly and with his back to the fire kept his eye on the group of men down at the creek. When he had finished, he walked down to the stream himself. A large man in the group fitted, in his hat and dress, Bucks's exact description. Scott had already spotted him an hour before, and stepped up to him now to arrest young John Rebstock.

He laid his hand on the man's shoulder and the man turned. But to Scott's surprise he was not the man wanted at all. He wore Rebstock's clothes and fitted Rebstock's description, but he was not Rebstock. The scout understood instantly how he had been tricked, but gave no sign.

Within the preceding thirty minutes the real Rebstock, whom Scott had already marked from his hiding-place in the canyon, had traded clothes with this man and, no doubt, made good his escape.

If Bob was chagrined, he made no sign.

"You must have made a good trade," he said, smiling at the teamster. "These clothes are a little big, but you will grow to them. How much boot did you get?"

Scott looked so slight and inoffensive that the teamster attempted insolence, and not only refused to answer questions, but threatened violence if the scout persisted in asking them. His companions crowding up encouraged him.

But numbers were not allowed for an instant to dominate the situation. Scott whipped a revolver from his belt, cocked it, and pressed it against the teamster's side. Dave Hawk loomed up in the moonlight and, catching by the collar one after another of the men crowding around Scott, Hawk, with his right hand or his left, whirled them spinning out of his way. If a man resisted the rough treatment, Hawk unceremoniously knocked him down and, drawing his own revolver, took his stand beside his threatened companion.

Other men came running up, the trader among them. A few words explained everything and the recalcitrant teamster concluded to speak. Scott, indeed, had but little to ask: he already knew the whole story. And when the teamster, threatened with search, pulled from his pocket a roll of bank-notes which he acknowledged had been given him for concealing the two fugitives and providing them with clothes, Scott released him—only notifying the trader incidentally that the man was robbing him and had loot, taken from the ammunition wagon, concealed under his blanket bales just searched. This information led to new excitement in the camp, and the Frenchman danced up and down in his wrath as he ordered the blanket wagon searched again. But his excitement did not greatly interest Scott and his party. They went their way and camped at some distance down the creek from their stirred-up neighbors.

Hawk and Bob Scott sat in the moonlight after the troopers had gone to sleep.

"They can't fool us very much longer," muttered Scott, satisfied with the day's work and taking the final disappointment philosophically, "until they can get horses they are chained to the ground in this country. There is only one place I know of where there are any horses hereabouts and that is Jack Casement's camp."

Hawk stretched himself out on the ground to sleep. "I'll tell you, Dave," continued Scott, "it is only about twenty miles from here to Casement's, anyway. Suppose I ride over there to-night and wire Stanley we've got track of the fellows. By the time you pick up the trail in the morning I will be back—or I may pick it up myself between here and the railroad. You keep on as far as Brushwood Creek and I'll join you there to-morrow by sundown."

It was so arranged. The night was clear and with a good moon the ride was not difficult, though to a man less acquainted with the mountains it would have been a hardship. Mile after mile Scott's hardy pony covered with no apparent effort. Bob did not urge him, and before midnight the white tents of the construction camp were visible in the moonlight. Scott went directly to the telegraph office, and after sending his message hunted up food and quarters for his beast and a sleeping-bunk for himself.

At daylight he was astir and sought breakfast before making inquiries and riding back to his party. On the edge of the camp stood a sort of restaurant, made up of a kitchen tent with a dismantled box-car body as an annex.

In this annex the food was served. It was entered from one side door, while the food was brought from the kitchen through the other side doorway of the car.

Into this crowded den Bob elbowed an unobtrusive way and seated himself in a retired corner. He faced the blind end of the car, and before him on the wall was tacked a fragment of a mirror in which he could see what was going on behind him. And without paying any apparent attention to anything that went on, nothing escaped him.

Next to where he sat, a breakfast of coffee and ham and eggs had been already served for somebody, apparently on an order previously given. At the opposite end of the car a small space was curtained off as a wash-room. Scott ordered his own breakfast and was slowly eating it when he noticed through the little mirror, and above and beyond the heads of the busy breakfasters along the serving-counter, a large man in the wash-room scrubbing his face vigorously with a towel.

Each time Scott looked up from his breakfast into the mirror the man redoubled his efforts to do a good job with the towel, hiding his face meantime well within its folds. The scout's curiosity was mildly enough aroused to impel him to watch the diligent rubbing with some interest. He saw, too, presently that the man was stealing glances out of his towel at him and yet between times intently rubbing his face.

This seemed odd, and Scott, now eying the man more carefully, noted his nervousness and wondered at it. However, he continued to enjoy his own meal. The waiter who had served him, hurried and impatient, also noticed the waiting breakfast untouched and called sharply to the man in the wash-room that his ham was served and, with scant regard for fine words, bade him come eat it.

This urgent invitation only added to the ill-concealed embarrassment of the stalling guest; but it interested the scout even more in the developing situation. Scott finished his breakfast and gave himself entirely over to watching in a lazy way the man who was making so elaborate a toilet.

There was no escape from either end of the car. That could be managed only through the side doors, which were too close to Scott to be available, and the scout, now fairly well enlightened and prepared, merely awaited developments.

He wanted to see the man come to his breakfast, and the man in the wash-room, combing his hair with vigor and peering anxiously through his own scrap of a mirror at Bob Scott, wanted to see the scout finish his coffee and leave the car. Scott, however, pounding ostentatiously on the table, called for a second cup of coffee and sipped it with apparent satisfaction. It was a game of cat and mouse— —with the mouse, in this instance, bigger than the cat, but as shy and reluctant to move as any mouse could be in a cat's presence. Scott waited until he thought the embarrassed man would have brushed the hair all out of his head, and at last, in spite of himself, laughed. As he did so, he turned half-way around on his stool and lifted his finger.

"Come, Rebstock," he smiled, calling to the fugitive. "Your breakfast is getting cold."

The man, turning as red as a beet, looked over the heads of those that sat between him and his tantalizing captor. But putting the best face he could on the dilemma and eying Scott nervously he walked over and, with evident reluctance, made ready to sit down beside him.

"Take your time," suggested Scott pleasantly. Then, as Rebstock, quite crestfallen, seated himself, he added: "Hadn't I better order a hot cup of coffee for you?" He took hold of the cup as he spoke, and looked hard at the gambler while making the suggestion.

"No, no," responded Rebstock, equally polite and equally insistent, as he held his hand over the cup and begged Scott not to mind. "This is all right."

"How was the walking last night?" asked Scott, passing the fugitive a big plate of bread. Rebstock lifted his eyes from his plate for the briefest kind of a moment.

"The—eh—walking? I don't know what you mean, captain. I slept here last night."

Scott looked under the table at his victim's boots. "John," he asked without a smile, "do you ever walk in your sleep?"

Rebstock threw down his knife and fork. "Look here, stranger," he demanded with indignation. "What do you want? Can't a man eat his breakfast in this place? I ask you," he demanded, raising his right hand with his knife in it as he appealed to the waiter, "can't a man eat his breakfast in this place without interruption?"

The waiter, standing with folded arms, regarded the two men without changing his stolid expression. "A man can eat his breakfast in this place without anything on earth except money. If you let your ham get cold because you were going to beat me out of the price, and you try to do it, I'll drag you out of here by the heels."

These unsympathetic words attracted the attention of every one and the breakfasters now looked on curiously but no one offered to interfere. Quarrels and disputes were too frequent in that country to make it prudent or desirable ever to intervene in one. A man considered himself lucky not to be embroiled in unpleasantness in spite of his best efforts to keep out. Rebstock turned again on his pursuer. "What do you want, anyhow, stranger?" he demanded fiercely. "A fight, I reckon."

"Not a bit of it. I want you, Rebstock," explained Scott without in the least raising his voice.

Rebstock's throaty tones seemed to contract into a wheeze. "What do you want me for?" he asked, looking nervously toward the other end of the car. As he did so, a man wearing a shirt and new overalls rose and started for the door. The instinct of Scott's suspicion fastened itself on the man trying to leave the place as being Rebstock's wanted companion.

Rising like a flash, he covered the second man with his pistol. "Hold on!" he exclaimed, pointing at him with his left hand. "Come over here!"

The man in overalls turned a calm face that showed nothing more than conscious innocence. But Scott was looking at his feet. His worn shoes were crusted heavily with alkali mud. "What do you want with me?" snarled the man halted at the door.

"I want you," said Scott, "for burning Point of Rocks station night before last. Here, partner," he continued, speaking to the waiter. "I'll pay for these two breakfasts; search that man for me," he continued, pointing to the man in the overalls.

"Search him yourself," returned the waiter stolidly. Scott turned like a wolf.

"What's that?" Another expression stole over his good-natured face. Holding his revolver to cover any one that resisted, he turned his accusing finger upon the insolent waiter. "You will talk to me, will you?" he demanded sharply. "Do as I tell you instantly, or I'll drive you out of camp and burn your shack to the ground. When I talk to you, General Jack Casement talks, and this railroad company talks. Search that man!"

Before the last word had passed his lips the waiter jumped over the counter and began turning the pockets of the man in the new overalls inside out. The fellow kept a good face even after a bunch of stolen railroad tickets were discovered in one pocket. "A man gave them to me last night to keep for him," he answered evenly.

"Never mind," returned Scott with indifference, "I will take care of them for him."

The news of the capture spread over the camp, and when Scott with his two prisoners walked across to General Casement's tent a crowd followed. Stanley had just arrived from Point of Rocks by train and was conferring with Casement when Scott came to the tent door. He greeted Bob and surveyed the captured fugitives.

"How did you get them?" he demanded.

Scott smiled and hung his head as he shook it, to anticipate compliments. "They just walked into my arms. Dave Hawk and the troopers are looking for these fellows now away down on Bitter Creek. They wandered into camp here last night to save us the trouble of bringing them. Isn't that it, Rebstock?"

Rebstock disavowed, but not pleasantly. He was not in amiable mood.

"What show has a fat man got to get away from anybody?" he growled.

CHAPTER XIX

When Hawk saw Bob Scott, two hours later, riding into his camp on the Brushwood with the two prisoners, he was taciturn but very much surprised.

Scott was disposed to make light of the lucky chance, as he termed it, that had thrown the two men into his way. Hawk, on the other hand, declared in his arbitrary manner that it was not wholly a lucky chance. He understood the Indian's dogged tenacity too well to think for a moment that the fugitives could have escaped him, even had he not ridden into Casement's camp as he so fortuitously had done.

The scout, Hawk knew, had the characteristic intuition of the frontiersman; the mental attributes that combine with keen observation and unusually good judgment as aids to success when circumstances are seemingly hopeless. Such men may be at fault in details, and frequently are, but they are not often wholly wrong in conclusions. And in their pursuit of a criminal they are like trained hounds, which may frequently lose their trail for a moment, but, before they have gone very far astray, come unerringly back to it.

"If they ever give you a chance, Bob, you will make a great thief-catcher," exclaimed Hawk with his naturally prodigal generosity of appreciation.

"I certainly never expected to catch Rebstock and this fellow Seagrue as easily as that," smiled Scott, as the troopers took charge of his men.

"If you hadn't caught them there you would have trailed them there. It would only have meant a longer chase."

"A whole lot longer."

"When you come to think of it, Bob, the railroad was their only hope, anyway. They did right in striking for it. Without horses, the big camp and the trains for Medicine Bend every day were their one chance to get away."

Scott assented. "The trouble with us," he smiled, "was that we didn't think until after it was all over. Sometime a man will come to these mountains who thinks things out before they happen instead of after. Then we will have a man fit to run the secret service on this railroad. But we are losing time," he added, tightening up his saddle girths.

"What are you going to do now? And why," demanded Hawk without waiting for an answer, "did you drag these men away down here instead of leaving them for Casement to lock up until we were ready to take them to Medicine Bend?"

"I am going to drag them farther yet," announced Scott. "I am going to ride after the French trader and fit these two fellows out in their own clothes again to make it easier for Bucks to indentify them."

84

"Don't say 'indentify,' Bob, say 'identify,'" returned Hawk testily.

Bob Scott usually turned away a sharp word with silence, and although he felt confident Hawk was wrong, he argued no further with him, but stuck just the same to his own construction of the troublesome word.

"You've got the right idea, Bob, if you have got the wrong word," muttered Hawk. "Why didn't you think of that sooner?"

They broke camp and started promptly. About noon they overtook the trading outfit and after some threatening forced the tricky teamster to rig the two gamblers out in their own apparel. Having done this, they started on a long ride for Casement's camp, reaching it again with their prisoners, and all very dusty and fatigued, long after dark.

The hard work voluntarily undertaken by the scout to aid the boy, as he termed Bucks, in identifying his graceless assailants was vindicated when, the next morning, the party with their prisoners arrived on a special train at Point of Rocks, and Bucks immediately pointed to Seagrue as the man who had first fired at him.

There were a few pretty hot moments on the platform when Bucks, among a group of five camp malefactors on their way to Medicine Bend, confronted the two men who had tried to kill him, and unhesitatingly pointed them out. Seagrue, tall and surly, denied vehemently ever having been at Point of Rocks and ever having seen Bucks. He declared the whole affair was "framed up" to send him to the penitentiary. He threatened if he were "sent up" to come back and kill Bucks if it was twenty years later—and did, in that respect, try to keep his word.

But his threats availed him nothing, and John Rebstock who, though still young, was a sly fox in crooked ways, contented himself with a philosophical denial of everything alleged against him, adding only in an injured tone that nobody would believe a fat man anyway.

It was he, however, rather than the less clever Seagrue, who had begun to excite sympathy for what he called his luckless plight and that of his companion, before they had left the railroad camp. Among the five evil-doers who had been rounded-up and deported for the jail at Medicine Bend, and now accompanied the two gamblers, Rebstock spread every story he could think of to arouse his friends at Medicine Bend to a demonstration in his behalf.

The very first efforts at putting civil law and order into effect were just then being tried in the new and lawless frontier railroad town and the contest between the two elements of decency and of license had reached an acute pass when Rebstock and Seagrue were thrown into jail at Medicine Bend. A case of sympathy for them was not hard to work up among men of their own kind and threats were heard up and down Front Street that if the railroading of two innocent men to the penitentiary were attempted something would happen.

Railroad men themselves, hearing the mutterings, brought word of them to head-quarters, but Stanley was in no wise disturbed. He had wanted to make an example for the benefit of the criminals who swarmed to the town, and now welcomed the chance to put the law's rigor on the men that had tried to assassinate his favorite operator. Bucks, lest he might be made the victim of a more successful attack, was brought down from Point of Rocks the first moment he could be relieved. A plot to put him out of the way, as the sole witness against the accused gamblers, was uncovered by Scott almost as soon as Bucks had returned to the big town and, warned by his careful friend, he rarely went up street except with a companion—most frequently with Scott himself.

As the day set for Rebstock's trial drew near, rumors were heard of a jail delivery. The jail itself was a flimsy wooden affair, and so crude in its appointments that any civilized man would have been justified in breaking out of it.

Nor was Brush, the sheriff, much more formidable than the jail itself. This official sought to curry favor with the townspeople—and that meant, pretty nearly, with the desperadoes—as well as to stand well with the railroad men; and in his effort to do both he succeeded in doing neither.

Bucks was given a night trick on his old wire in the local station, and in spite of the round of excitement about him settled down to the routine of regular work. The constant westbound movement of construction material made his duties heavier than before, but he seemed able to do whatever work he was assigned to and gained the reputation of being dependable, wherever put.

He had risen one night from his key, after despatching a batch of messages, to stir the fire—the night was frosty—when he heard an altercation outside on the platform. In another moment the waiting-room door was thrown open and Bucks turned from the stove, poker in hand, to see a man in the extremity of fear rush into his lonely office.

The man, hatless and coatless and evidently trying to escape from some one, was so panic-stricken that his eyes bulged from their sockets, and his beard was so awry that it was a moment before Bucks recognized his old acquaintance Dan Baggs.

"They are after me, Bucks," cried Baggs, closing the door in desperation. "They will kill me—hide me or they'll kill me."

Before the operator could ask a question in explanation, almost before the words were out of the frightened engineman's mouth, and with Bucks pointing with his poker to the door, trying to tell Baggs to lock it, the door again flew open and Bucks saw the face of a Front Street confidence man bursting through it.

Bucks sprang forward to secure the door behind the intruder, but he was too late even for that. Half a dozen more men crowded into the room. To ask questions was useless; every one began talking at once. Baggs, paralyzed with fear, cowered behind the stove and the confidence man, catching sight of him, tried to crowd through the wicket gate. As he sprang toward it, Bucks confronted him with his poker.

"Let that gate alone or I'll brain you," he cried, hardly realizing what he was saying, but well resolved what to do.

The gambler, infuriated, pointed to Baggs. "Throw that cur out here," he yelled.

Baggs, now less exposed to his enemies, summoned the small remnant of his own courage and began to abuse his pursuer.

"LET THAT GATE ALONE OR I'LL BRAIN YOU," HE CRIED.

Bucks, between the two men with his poker, tried to stop the din long enough to get information. He drew the enraged gambler into a controversy of words and used the interval to step to his key. As he did so, Baggs, catching up a monkey-wrench that Bucks ordinarily used on his letter-press, again defied his enemy.

87

It was only a momentary burst of courage, but it saved the situation. Taking advantage of the instant, Bucks slipped the fingers of his left hand over the telegraph key and wired the despatchers upstairs for help. It was none too soon. The men, leaning against the railing, pushed it harder all along the line. It swayed with an ominous crack and the fastening gave way. Baggs cowered. His pursuers yelled, and with one more push the railing crashed forward and the confidence man sprang for the engineer. Baggs ran back to where Bucks stood before his table, and the latter, clutching his revolver, warned Baggs's pursuers not to lay a hand on him.

Defying the single-handed defender, the gambler whipped out his own pistol to put an end to the fight. It was the signal for his followers, and in another minute half a dozen guns covered Bucks and his companion.

Seconds meant minutes then. Bucks understood that only one shot was needed as the signal for his own destruction. What he did not quite realize was that the gambler confronting him and his victim read something in Bucks's eye that caused him to hesitate. He felt that if a shot were fired, whatever else happened, it would mean his own death at Bucks's hand. It was this that restrained him, and the instant saved the operator's life.

He heard the clattering of feet down the outside stairway, and the next moment through the open door on the run dashed Bill Dancing, swinging a piece of iron pipe as big as a crowbar. The yardmaster, Callahan, was at his heels, and the two, tearing their way through the room, struck without mercy.

The thugs crowded to the door. The narrow opening choked with men trying to dodge the blows rained upon them by Dancing and Callahan. Before Baggs could rub his eyes the room was cleared, and half a dozen trainmen hastily summoned and led by a despatcher were engaged out upon the platform in a free fight with the Front Street ruffians.

Within the office, the despatcher found Bucks talking to Callahan, while Baggs was trying to explain to Bill Dancing how the confidence men had tried to inveigle him into a "shell" game and, when they found they could not rob him of his month's pay in any other way, had knocked him down to pick his pockets.

Callahan, who knew the trouble-making element better than any of the railroad men, went up town to estimate the feeling after the fight, which was now being discussed by crowds everywhere along Front Street. For every bruised and sore head marked by the punishment given by Dancing in the defence of Baggs a new enemy and an active one had been made.

Stanley came in late from the west and heard the story of the fight. His comment was brief but significant. "It will soon be getting so they won't wait for the railroad men to draw their pay. They will come down here," said he ironically, "to draw it for them."

CHAPTER XX

A second and more serious disturbance followed close on the fight at the railroad station. A passenger alighting in the evening from a westbound train was set upon, robbed, and beaten into insensibility within ten feet of the train platform. A dozen other passengers hastened to his assistance. They joined in repulsing his assailants and were beating them off when other thugs, reinforcing their fellows, attacked the passengers and those railroad men that had hurried up to drive off the miscreants.

In the mêlée, a brakeman was shot through the head and a second passenger wounded. But the railroad men rallied and, returning the pistol fire, drove off the outlaws.

The train was hurried out of town and measures were taken at once to defend the railroad property for the night. Guards were set in the yards, and a patrol established about the roundhouse, the railroad hotel and the eating-house and freight-houses.

Stanley, with his car attached to the night passenger train, was on his way to Casement's camp when the fight occurred, and had taken Bucks with him. The despatch detailing the disturbance reached him at a small station east of Point of Rocks, where he was awakened and the message was read to him advising the manager of the murder of the brakeman.

A freight-train, eastbound, stood on the passing track. Stanley roused Bucks and, notifying the despatchers, ordered the engine cut off from the freight-train, swung up into the cab, and started for Medicine Bend. As they pulled out, light, Stanley asked for every notch of speed the lumbering engine could stand, and Oliver Sollers, the engineman, urged the big machine to its limit.

The new track, laid hastily and only freshly ballasted, was as rough as corduroy, and the lurching of the big diamond stack made the cab topple at every rail joint. But Sollers was not the runner to lose nerve under difficulties and did not lessen the pressure on the pistons. If Stanley, determined and silent, his lips set and hanging on for dear life as the cab jumped and swung under him, felt any qualms at the dangerous pace he had asked for, he betrayed none. With Bucks, open-eyed with surprise, hanging on in front of him, Stanley gave no heed to the bouncing, and the freight-engine pounded through the mountains like a steam-roller with a touch of crushed-stone delirium. Hour after hour the wild pace was kept up through the Sleepy Cat Mountains and across the Sweet Grass Plains. There was no easing up until the frantic machine struck the gorge of the Medicine River and whistled for the long yards above the roundhouse.

Things had so quieted down by the time Stanley, springing up the stairs two steps at a time, reached the despatchers' office, that they were sorry they had sent in such haste for him. Stanley himself had no regrets. He knew better than those about him the temper of the crowd he had to deal with and felt that he needed every minute to prepare for what he had to do. Bucks was sent to bring in Dancing, Bob Scott, and the more resolute among the railroad men. A brief consultation was held, and the attitude of the gamblers carefully discussed.

Scott, who had been up town since the murder, had collected sufficient proof that the chief outlaw, Levake, had done the shooting, and Stanley now sent Scott to Brush, the sheriff, with a verbal message demanding Levake's arrest.

Every man that heard the order given knew what it meant. Every one that listened realized it was the beginning of a fight in which there could be no retreat for Stanley; that it would be a fight to a finish, and that no man could say where it would end.

Bob Scott hitched his trousers at the word from his sandy-haired chief. For Bob, orders meant orders and the terror of Levake's name in Medicine Bend had no effect on him.

"You might as well ask a jack-rabbit to tackle a mountain lion as to try to get Brush to arrest Levake," declared Dave Hawk cynically.

But Stanley's hand struck the table like a hammer: "We are going to have a show-down here. We will go through the forms; this is the beginning—and I am going to follow it to the end. Either Levake has got to quit the town or I have."

Dave Hawk looked around with a new idea. He bent his eyes on Bob: "Better get Brush to deputize *you* to make the arrest."

"That is it!" exclaimed Stanley. "Get him to deputize you, Bob, and we will clean up this town as it hasn't been cleaned since the flood."

Scott shook his head: "I don't believe Brush has the sand for that. We will see."

Up Front Street, through the various groups of men still discussing the events of the evening, Scott, followed only by Bill Dancing, made his way, nodding and patiently or pleasantly grinning as the greetings or ridicule of the crowd were thrown at him. He went to the rooms of the sheriff only to find them locked, and made his way down town again looking through the resorts in a search for Brush.

After much trouble, he found him at a gaming-table, inclined to appear sceptical as to the story that Levake had killed an unoffending brakeman. When Scott repeated Stanley's demand that Levake be arrested, the sheriff slammed down his cards and declared he would not be made a cat's-paw for any man; that the brakeman, according to accounts reaching him, had been killed in a fair fight and he would hear no more of it. Then, as if his game had been unreasonably interfered with and his peace of mind injured, he rose from the table to relieve his annoyance.

Meantime Bill Dancing slipped into his vacated seat, picked up the discarded hand of cards and announced it was too good to throw away. "Will anybody," Bill asked dryly, "play the hand with me while Brush is arresting Levake?" The laugh of Brush's own companions at this proposal stung him as an imputation of his cowardice, and he made an additional display of rage to counteract the unconcealed contempt in which his cronies held him.

He turned on Scott angrily. "Go arrest the man yourself, if you want him," he thundered.

Scott snapped up the suggestion. He pointed a lean finger at the shifty peace officer. "Deputize me to do it, if you dare, Brush!" he softly exclaimed, fixing his brown eyes on the flushed face of the coward.

Not a man in the room moved or spoke. Brush saw himself trapped. Scott's finger called for an answer and the sheriff found no escape. "I knew you hadn't the nerve to give me a deputy's badge," laughed Scott, to spur the man's lagging courage; "you are too afraid of Levake."

The taunt had its effect. Brush raved about his courage, and Bill Dancing, slapping him ferociously on the back, convinced him that he really was a brave man. Taken volubly in tow by the two railroad emissaries, who were far from being as simple as they seemed, Brush returned to his lodgings at the jail to issue the coveted paper authorizing Scott to serve any warrants in his stead.

Before the ink was dry on the certificate the word had gone down Front Street, and the town knew that Levake's arrest was in prospect. As Dancing and Scott left the jail and walked down to the station, they were surrounded by a curious throng of men watching for further developments in the approaching crisis of the struggle with outlawry in the railroad town.

The night was far advanced, but a third element was now to make itself felt in the situation. The decent business men had already seen the approach of the storm and resolved on protecting their own interests, which they realized were on the side of law and order. Word had been passed from one to another of a proposed meeting. It was held toward daybreak in a secret place. One and all present were pledged to act together under a leadership then and there agreed upon, and after so organizing, with a resolute merchant named Atkinson at their head, and with a quiet that foreboded no good to the gamblers and outlaws, the men who had gone to the rendezvous as business men left it as vigilantes, banded together to defend their rights and property against the lawless element that had terrorized legitimate business.

In the morning secret word was brought by Atkinson to Stanley of the resolve of the new allies to stand by him in his efforts to rid the town of its undesirables for good and all. It was welcome intelligence, and the railroad chief assured the plucky merchant of his hearty cooperation in the designs of the newly constituted law-and-order committee.

"When the machinery of the law has miserably failed to protect our lives and property," he said concisely, "we have nothing left for it but to protect them ourselves." Arms had been telegraphed for and every effort made to secure troops in the emergency. But the Indian uprising had taken every available infantryman and trooper into the north and there was not now sufficient time to get them together for action. The railroad men, Stanley knew, must depend on themselves and upon such assistance as the decent element in the town could render.

Meantime the outlaws were not idle. They spent the day whipping the gamblers and their hangers-on into line, upon the prediction that if they themselves were dispersed scant quarter would be shown their disorderly associates.

Scott spent the day leisurely. Stanley had asked him not to move until his own arrangements for a defensive fight were completed. That the outlaws had secret sources of information even in the railroad circles, came out startlingly. A special train—an express car pulled by an engine—entered the railroad yard at dusk that evening, when a party of men running out from the cover of the freight warehouse attempted to rush it for arms and ammunition.

They were met at the car doors by six of the best men that could be picked up along the line during the day run of the special across the plains. Stanley had wired instructions to head-quarters to send him six men that feared neither smoke nor powder, and six stalwarts taken on at Grand Island, North Platte, and Julesburg guarded the car and tumbled like cats out of a bag upon the surprised raiders.

The encounter was spirited, but it took only a moment to convince the assaulting party that they had made a mistake. Clubbing their heavy revolvers, the guards, any one of whom in close quarters could account for two ordinary men, threw themselves from the car step directly into the crowd and struck right and left. There was no regard for persons, and in the half-dark the Medicine Bend ruffians, surprised and confused, were soon fighting one another.

But one-sided as the contest was, it did not go fast enough to suit the guards, who, seizing the clubs thrown away by the rabble, charged them in a line and drove them up the street. Railroad men who came running from the station to help were too late. The flurry was over and they found nothing to do but to cheer their new aids.

Nor were the gamblers asleep. Word had gone out both east and west of the approaching crisis between the disorderly and the law-and-order elements, and every passenger train into Medicine Bend brought mysterious men from towns and railroad camps who were openly or secretly allied in one or another vicious calling to the classes that were now making a stand for the rule or ruin of the railroad town.

A mob of sympathizers gathered in Front Street to protect from further punishment the party that had tried to capture the express car. But the railroad men had no idea of pursuing the raiders beyond the yard limits, and indeed were restrained by strict orders from doing so. Stanley sent word immediately to the sheriff, demanding the arrest of the new peace-disturbers, but the sheriff no longer made a pretence of arresting law-breakers. In Front Street, the mob, emboldened by their apparent control of the situation and increasing in clamor and numbers, were now in a humor for anything that promised pillage or vengeance. There were still among them a few cool-headed criminals who counselled caution, but these were hooted down by men who had never tasted the rigor of vigilante rule.

Out of a dozen wild schemes broached by as many wild heads of the excited crowd, in which were now lined up for any lawlessness all the idlers, floaters, the improvident, and the reckless elements of a frontier gambling town, one caught the popular fancy. Some one proposed a jail delivery to release Rebstock and Seagrue, persecuted by the railroad company. The idea spread like wildfire, and a score of men, reinforced by more at every door as they proceeded up Front Street, made their way to the jail.

Fast as they came, time was given for word to the sheriff, who conveniently got out of the way, and, led by half a dozen men with crowbars and spike-mauls, the outlaws surrounded and overran the jail yard and without a show of resistance from any one began smashing in the entrance and battering down the cell doors.

The first suggestion included only the delivery of the two men. But this was effected so easily that more was undertaken. The jail at Medicine Bend, being the only one within many miles in any direction, harbored the criminals of the whole mountain region, and these now cried to friendly ears for their own freedom. Cell after cell was battered open and the released criminals, snatching tools from the mob, led in the fight to free their fellows. In less than half an hour every cell had been emptied and a score of hardened malefactors had been added to the mob, which now proposed to celebrate the success of its undertaking by setting fire to the jail itself.

The vigilantes down town, though taking the alarm, had moved too slowly. A jail delivery meant, they knew, that their stores would be looted, and, under the leadership of Atkinson, they attempted to avert the mischief impending.

Gathering twenty-five determined men, they started with a shout for the hill, only to see the sky already lighting with the flames of the burning building. The mob, not understanding at first, welcomed the new-comers with a roar of approval.

But they were soon undeceived. The vigilantes began to try to save the jail and their efforts brought about the first clash of a night destined long to be remembered in Medicine Bend. The brawlers in the crowd stayed to fight the vigilantes. The thieves and night-birds fell away in the darkness, and like black cats scurried down town to pillage the stores and warehouses of the fire-fighters on the hill.

The few clerks and watchmen defending the stores, these knaves made short work of. Dancing and Scott, with Stanley, Bucks, and a party of railroad men, uneasy at the reports from the jail and now able to see the sky reddening with the flames, moved in and out of the gloom of side streets to keep track of the alarming situation and were the earliest to discover the looting movement.

A convenient general store at Front and Hill Streets was the first to be pillaged. Dancing wanted to lead a party against the looters, but Stanley pointed out the folly of half a dozen men trying to police the whole street.

"We can do nothing here, Bill. Those vigilantes have no business on the hill. Get word to them, if you can, that the stores are being robbed. They can't save the jail; they ought to come back and save their own property. I can't bring men up from the roundhouse. We've got to protect our own property first. If we could get word to them—but a man never could get through that mob to the jail."

93

"I reckon I can, colonel," said Bill Dancing, throwing off his coat.

"They will kill you, Bill," predicted Stanley.

"No," growled the lineman, rolling up his shirt sleeves. "Not me. I wouldn't stand for it."

CHAPTER XXI

Slipping away behind the long warehouses in Front Street and moving swiftly in and out of friendly shadows on his long journey up the hill, Dancing started for the jail. He was hardly more than well under way when he was aware of one following him and, turning to fell him with his fist, he started as he found it was Bucks.

The latter confronted him coolly: "Go ahead, Bill; I am going with you."

"Who said you could go?" exclaimed the lineman. "You can't. Go back!"

Bucks stood his ground.

"Do you want to get killed?" thundered Dancing hotly.

"Two are better than one on a job like this," returned Bucks, without giving way. "Go on, will you?"

With a volley of grumbling objections, Dancing at length directed Bucks to stick close to him, whatever happened, and to fight the best he could in case they were cornered.

Ahead of them the glare of the conflagration lighted the sky and the air was filled with the shouts of the mob surrounding the fighting vigilantes. Only half a block away, men were hurrying up and down Front Street, while the two clambered along the obscure and half-opened street leading to the jail and parallel to the main thoroughfare.

Dancing, to whom every foot of the rocky way was familiar and who could get over obstructions in the dark as well as if it were day, led the way with a celerity that kept his companion breathing fast. Both had long legs, but Dancing in some mysterious way planted his feet with marvellous certainty of effect, while Bucks slipped and floundered over rocks and brush piles and across gullies until they took a short cut through a residence yard and found themselves on the heels of the mob surrounding the burning jail and in the glare of the fire in upper Front Street.

"Stick close, sonny," muttered the lineman, "we must push through these fellows before they reco'nize us."

He stooped as he spoke and picked up a piece of hickory—the broken handle of a spike-maul. "Railroad property anyway," he muttered. "It might come handy. But gum shoes for us now till we are forced. Perhaps we can sneak all the way through."

Without further ado Dancing, with Bucks on his heels, elbowed his way into the crowd. The outer fringe of this he knew was not dangerous, being made up chiefly of onlookers. But in another minute the two were in the midst of a yelling, swaying mix-up between the aggressive mob and a thin fringe of vigilantes, who, hard-pressed, had abandoned the jail to its fate and were trying to fight their way down town.

Dancing, like a war-horse made suddenly mad by smoke of battle, throwing caution and strategy to the winds, suddenly released a yell and began to lay about him. His appearance in the fray was like that of a bombshell timed to explode in its midst. The slugging gamblers turned in astonishment on the new fighting man, but they were not long left in doubt as to which cause he espoused. In the next instant they were actively dodging his flashing club, and the vigilantes encouraged as if by an angel fought with fresh vigor.

Bucks was stunned by the suddenness of Bill's change of tactics. It was evident that he had completely forgotten his mission and now meant to enjoy himself in the unequal fray that he had burst in upon. The vigilantes cried a welcome to their new ally. But one cry rose above every other and that was from Dancing's own throat as he laid about with his club.

Consternation seized the rioters and they were thrown for a moment into confusion. They then recognized Dancing and a shout went up.

"Railroad men!" cried a dozen of the mob at once.

And above these cries came one wheezing but stentorian voice: "You've got 'em now; finish 'em!"

Bucks knew that voice. It was Rebstock.

The crowd took up the cry, but the lineman, swinging right and left with terrific strength and swiftness, opened a way ahead of him while Bucks kept close by till Dancing had cut through to the vigilantes. Then, turning with them as they raised their own cry of triumph, Dancing helped to drive the discomfited rioters back.

It was only for a moment that the vigilantes held their advantage. Outnumbering the little band, the rioters closed in on their flanks and showered stones upon them. Bill Dancing was the centre of the fight. A piece of rock laid open his scalp, but, though the mob was sure of getting him, he fought like a whirlwind. They redoubled their efforts to bring him down. One active rioter with the seam of some other fight slashed across his forehead struck down a vigilante and ran in on Dancing. It was Seagrue. The lineman, warned by Bucks, turned too late to escape a blow on the head that would have dazed a bullock. But Dancing realized the instant he received the blow that Seagrue had delivered it.

He whirled like a wounded bear and sprang at Seagrue, taking upon his shoulder a second blow hardly less terrific than the first. Before Seagrue could strike again, Dancing was upon him. Tearing at each other's throats the two men struggled, each trying to free his right arm. Seagrue was borne steadily backward. Then the lineman's big arm shot upward and down like a trip-hammer and Seagrue sunk limp to the ground.

The vigilantes themselves, profiting by the momentary diversion, got away. Bucks had seen the peril of being separated from their friends, but he was powerless to avert it. As Dancing struck Seagrue down, his enemies closed in

95

behind the moving vigilantes. Bucks fought his way to the lineman's side and in another instant the two were beset. Dancing, hard-pressed, made a dash to break through the circle to liberty. Half a dozen men sprang at him, and trampling Bucks completely under foot aimed their blows at his defender.

Dancing saw Bucks fall and, clubbing his way to his side, caught Bucks from the ground by the coat collar, and dragging him with his left hand, swung with his right hand his deadly club. Nothing less would have saved them. The fight, moving every instant after Dancing, reached the broad wooden steps leading from the jail yard to the street. Down these the lineman, stubborn and bleeding, drove a desperate way. And Bucks, able again to handle himself, was putting up a good fight when, to his horror, Dancing, fighting down the flight of steps, stumbled and fell.

Half a dozen men, with a yell, jumped for him. Bucks thought the finish had come. He sprang into the fight and, armed only with a wagon spoke, cracked right and left wherever he could reach a head. Dancing he had given over for dead, when to his astonishment the lineman rose out of the heap about him, shaking off his enemies like rats.

Flames shooting up from the burning jail lighted the scene. Dancing, bare-headed, and with only a part of his shirt hanging in ribbons from his left arm, his hair matted in blood across his forehead and his eyes blazing, was a formidable sight. He had lost his club but he was at no loss for a weapon. It was said of Bill Dancing in later days that he could lift a thirty-foot steel rail. Bucks saw him now catch up a man scrambling in front of him and swing him by the legs like a battering ram. With this victim, he mowed down men like corks, and, flinging the man at last bodily into the faces of his friends, he started like a deer up Cliff Street with Bucks at his heels.

Sure that they now had him, the rioters followed in a swarm. Cliff Street, only a block long and only half-opened, terminated then at the cliffs above the gorge of the Medicine River. But darkness under the brow of the hill helped the fleeing railroad men. Dancing dodged in and out of the undergrowth that fringed the street line and eluding his pursuers reached the brow of the cliff unseen. The rioters, knowing that no escape lay in that direction, beat the bushes that fringed the half-opened street, confident that the fugitives were in hiding among them.

For an ordinary man, indeed, there was no escape toward the river. A wall of rock fell a hundred feet to the water's edge. The crowd, growing every moment as the word passed that Dancing was whipped, left the hunted man and his companion little time for decision. Dancing, in truth, needed but little. His purpose was fixed the instant he saw himself cut off from every other chance. He halted only on the brink of the precipice itself. Catching Bucks's arm, he told him hurriedly what they must do and cautioned him. "It's the last chance, sonny," he murmured, as his iron fingers gripped the boy's arm. "We can make it—if you do exactly as I tell you."

The gathering cries closed in behind them while they were taking off their shoes. Creeping on his hands and knees along the brow of the cliff, Dancing felt out his location with his fingers. And with that sixth sense of instinct which rises to a faculty when dangers thicken about a resolute man, the lineman found what he sought.

He caught at the root of a rock-bound cedar, swung himself over the cliff, and called to Bucks to follow. Bucks acted wholly on faith. The blackness below was impenetrable, and perhaps better so, since he could not see what he was undertaking. Only the roar of the river came up from the depths. It sounded a little ominous as Bucks, grasping the cedar root, swung over and after an agonizing instant felt a support for his feet. He stood on a ledge of rock so narrow that it gave only a footing even in daylight, but Bucks was called on to descend it in the middle of the night.

For any man to have attempted the feat seemed to him, the next morning, sheer insanity. Dancing, however, knew the treacherous face of the river wall. To his gigantic size and strength he united the sureness of a cat in climbing up or down a mountain arête. Often he had crept with a telegraph wire, unaided, where his best men hung back even in harness. There was, in fact, no time now for halting. The rioters, eager on the trail, were calling for torches, and, if discovered before they reached the water, the lives of the two men would be snuffed out by dropping rocks on their heads.

Flattening himself as he had been bidden to do and with his cheek laid to the face of the sheer rock, clasping from time to time with his outstretched left hand such slight uneven surfaces as he could feel, Bucks moved to the right after Dancing, who gripped his extended right hand and led him foot by foot down the perilous way. Not a word was spoken, hardly a breath drawn, as the lineman felt for his slippery foothold with the deftness of a gorilla, and, pressing Bucks's hand as the signal to take a follow step, he made a slow but steady descent.

The roar of the river already sounded in Bucks's ears like a cataract, but the shock of extreme danger had numbed his apprehension. Chips of the sharp granite cut his feet like knives, and he knew that the sticky feeling upon his bare soles was blood oozing through the broken skin. He had already given up expectation of ever leaving the gorge alive and merely responded to his companion's will. The one thought that came to his mind was curiosity as to what Dancing ever expected to do if they reached the bottom without accident.

Suddenly above the roar of the river he heard the muffled crack of fire-arms coming as if out of another world. He wondered whether they themselves were already being fired at, but experienced nothing more than curiosity in the thought. Only the pressure of the big hand that gripped his own impressed itself powerfully upon his consciousness, and at each squeeze he put his foot forward mechanically, intent on a dull resolve to obey orders.

He presently felt a new signal from the long fingers that wound around his own. He tried to answer by stepping, but Dancing whose face was turned away, restrained him. Then it flashed on Bucks that the lineman was signalling Morse to him, and that the dot-and-dash squeezes meant: "Half-way down. Half-way down."

Bucks answered with one word: "Hurrah!" But he squeezed it along the nerves and muscles like lightning.

97

He could hear the labored breathing of his companion as he strained at intervals every particle of his strength to reach a new footing of safety. Every vine and scrubby bush down the cliff wall was tested for its strength and root, and Dancing held Bucks's hand so that he could instantly release it if he himself should plunge to death.

Bucks had already been told that if this happened he must hang as long as he could without moving and if he could hold on till daylight he would be rescued by railroad men. All this was going through his head when, responding to a signal to step down, and, unable to catch some word that Dancing whispered, he stretched his leg so far that he lost his balance. He struggled to recover. Dancing called again sharply to him, but he was too wrought up to understand. Dizziness seized him, and resigning himself, with an exclamation, to death, he felt himself dropping into space.

In the next instant he was caught in Dancing's arms:

"Gosh darn it, why didn't you jump, as I told you?" exclaimed the lineman, setting him up on his feet. "You pretty near clean upset us both."

"Where are we, Bill?" muttered Bucks, swallowing his shock.

"Right here at the water, and them fellows up there beating the bush for us. There's shooting down town, too. Some new deviltry. How good a swimmer are you, Bucks? By gum, I forgot to ask you before you started."

"I can swim better than I can climb, Bill."

"We've only a quarter of a mile and downstream at that. And the current here would float a keg of nails."

"How about rocks, Bill?" asked Bucks, peering dubiously toward the roar of the rushing river.

"All up-stream from here," returned Dancing, edging down the shelving table toward the water. "Lock arms with me so I don't lose you, sonny. What in Sam Hill is that?"

Far down the river the two saw a tongue of flame leaping into the sky. They watched it for a moment. Dancing was the first to locate the conflagration, which grew now, even as they looked, by leaps and bounds. The two stood ready to plunge into the river when a fire of musketry echoed up the gorge. The lineman clutched Bucks's arm.

"There's fighting going on down there now. What's that smokestack? By Jing, the roundhouse is on fire!"

CHAPTER XXII

They plunged together into the river. The water, icy cold, was a shock, but Dancing had made no mistake. They were below the rocks and needed only to steady themselves as the resistless current swept them down toward the railroad yards.

Bucks demonstrated that he could swim and the two seemed hardly in the water before they could fully see the burning roundhouse. A moment later, chilled to the bone but with his mind cleared by the sharp plunge, Bucks felt his companion's arm drawing him toward the farther shore where, in the slack water of an elbow of the stream, Dancing led the way across a shoal of gravel and Bucks waded after him up the riverbank.

They hastened together across the dark railroad yard. The sound of firing came again from the square in front of the railroad station and thither they directed their fleeing feet. To the right they heard the shouts of the men who were fighting the fire at the roundhouse and the hot crackling of the flames. They reached the station together and entered the waiting-room by a rear door.

Men were running everywhere in and out of the building and the waiting-room was barricaded for war. Bill Dancing caught a passing trainman by the arm.

"What's going on here?"

The man looked at the lineman and his companion in surprise: "The gamblers are driving the vigilantes, Bill. They've got all Front Street. What's the matter with you?"

Dancing caught sight of Bob Scott coming down the rear stairway with an armful of rifles, and, without answering the question, called to him.

"Hello!" exclaimed Scott halting. He started as he saw Bucks. "Were *you* with him? And I've been scouring the town for you! Stanley will have a word to say to you, youngster. They thought the gamblers had you, Bill," he added, turning to the lineman.

Dancing, a sight from the pounding he had taken, his clothing in tatters, and with the blood-stains now streaked by the water dripping from his hair, drew himself up. "I hope you didn't think so, Bob? Did they reckon a handful of blacklegs would get me?"

Scott grinned inscrutably. "They've got the best part of your shirt, Bill. How did you get off?"

"Swam for it," muttered Dancing, shaking himself. "Where's Stanley?"

"Out behind the flat cars. He is arming the vigilantes. We've fenced off the yards with loaded freight-cars. They've fired the roundhouse on us, but the rifles and ammunition that came to-night are upstairs here. Take some of these guns, Bill, and hand them around in front. Bucks can follow you with a box of ammunition."

Scott spoke hurriedly and ran out of the door facing Front Street Square. A string of flat cars had been run along the house-track in front of the station, and behind these the hard-pressed vigilantes, reinforced now by the railroad men, were taking up a new line of defence. Driven through the town in a running battle, they were in straits when they reached Stanley's barricade.

Following a resolve already well defined, the railroad chief conferred with the vigilante leaders for a brief moment. He called them to his office and denounced the folly of half-way measures.

"You see," said Stanley, pointing to two dead men whom the discomfited business men had brought off with them, "what temporizing has done. There is only one way to treat with these people." He was interrupted by firing from across the square. "In an hour they will have every store in Front Street looted."

The deliberation for a few moments was a stormy one, but Stanley held his ground. "Desperate diseases, gentlemen," he said, addressing Atkinson and his companions, "require desperate remedies, and you must sometime come to what I propose."

"What you propose," returned Atkinson gloomily, "will ruin us."

Stanley answered with composure: "You are ruined now. What you should consider is whether, if you don't cut this cancer of gambling, outlawry, and murder out while you have a chance, it won't remain to plague you as long as you do business in Medicine Bend, and remain to ruin you periodically. This is always going to be a town and a big one. As long as this railroad is operated, this ground where we stand is and must be the chief operating point for the whole mountain division. You and I may be wiped out of existence and the railroad will go on as before. But it is for you to accept or reject what I propose as the riddance of this curse to your community.

"The railroad has been drawn into this fight by assault upon its men. It can meet violence with violence and protect itself, or it can temporarily abandon a town where protection is not afforded its lives and property. In an emergency, trains could be run through Medicine Bend without stopping. The right of way could be manned with soldiers. But the railroad can't supply men enough to preserve in your town the law and order which you yourselves ought to preserve. And if we were compelled to build division facilities, temporarily, elsewhere, while they would ultimately come back here, it might be years before they did so. What else but your ruin would this mean?"

He had hardly ceased speaking when the conference was broken in upon. Bob Scott ushered in two men sent under a flag of truce from the rioters. The offer they brought was that Rebstock and Seagrue should be surrendered, provided Stanley would give his personal pledge that the two should not be shot but sent out of town until peace was restored, and that they should be accorded a fair trial when brought back.

Stanley listened carefully to all that was said:

"Who sent you?" he demanded.

"The committee up street," returned the envoys evasively.

"You mean Levake sent you," retorted Stanley. He sat at his desk and eyed the two ruffians, as they faced him somewhat nervously. They at length admitted that they had come from Levake, and gave Stanley his chance for an answer.

"Tell Levake for me there will be no peace for him or his until he comes down here with his hands behind his back. When I want Rebstock and Seagrue I will let him know. I want him first," said Stanley, dismissing the messengers without more ado.

CHAPTER XXIII

He had resolved that Levake was to be punished, but it was not a unanimous voice that backed the railroad leader in his determination. Weak-kneed men in the conference wanted to compromise and end the fight where it stood. Even Atkinson was disposed to make terms, as the party returned to the barricade.

"No," repeated Stanley. "Levake is the head and front of this whole disorder. As long as he can shoot down unarmed men in the streets of Medicine Bend there will be no law and order here. While men see him walking these streets unpunished they will take their cue from him and rob and shoot whom they please—Levake and his ilk must go. A railroad, on the start, brings a lawless element with it—this is true. But it also brings law and order and that element has come to Medicine Bend to stay. If the machinery of the law is too weak to support it, so much worse for the machinery. I don't want to see blood shed or property destroyed, but the responsibility for this rests with the outlaws that are terrorizing this town. And I will spend every ounce of ammunition I have and fight them to the last man, rather than compromise with a bunch of cutthroats.

"If any man here feels differently about this, he may step out of the barricade now," continued Stanley, addressing those of the townsmen that listened. "There will be no hard feeling. But this is the time to do it. Worse is ahead of us before we can clean the town up as it will have to be cleaned sometime. The longer you leave the job undone, the harder it will be when you tackle it."

A movement across the square interrupted his words, and a messenger waving a white handkerchief came over to the barricade to ask for a surgeon for a wounded man. There were some who opposed sending any relief to men that had forfeited all claim to humane consideration. Doctor Arnold, however, was summoned, and Stanley finally determined that the matter should be left to the surgeon himself—he could go if he wished. Arnold did not hesitate in his decision. "It is my duty to go," he decided briefly.

"I don't quite see that," muttered Atkinson.

The white-haired surgeon turned to the leader of the vigilantes. "It is not a matter of personal inclination, Atkinson. When I took my degree for the practice of medicine, I took an oath to respond to every call of suffering and I have no right to refuse this one."

Leaving his own injured with his assistant, the surgeon told the messenger to proceed and the two walked across the square and up Front Street to the Three Horses. Arriving there, Arnold was asked to dress the wound of a man that had been shot through the breast in the fight along Fort Street. While he was working over his patient, who lay on a table surrounded by a motley crowd of onlookers, Levake walked in. He nodded to the surgeon and drawing a pocket knife, while Arnold was cleansing the wound, sat down beside him to whittle a stick.

"I hear your man, Stanley, wants me," began Levake after an interval.

"I guess you hear right," returned Arnold dryly.

"Tell him for me to come get me, will you?" suggested Levake.

"If he ever comes after you, Levake, he will get you," returned Arnold, looking the outlaw straight in the eye. "There isn't any doubt about that," he added, resuming his task.

Levake whittled but made no reply. He watched the surgeon's work closely, and when Arnold had finished and given directions for the wounded man's care he walked out of the place with him.

"Tell Stanley what I said, will you?" repeated Levake, as the railroad surgeon left the door and started down street.

Arnold made no answer and Levake, taunting him to send all the men the railroad had after him, followed Arnold toward the square.

The surgeon understood that it was Levake's purpose to engage him in a dispute and kill him if he could. Arnold, moreover, was hot-tempered and made no concealment of his feelings toward any man. For this reason, despite his realization of danger, he was an easy prey.

To the final taunt of the outlaw the surgeon made rather a sharp answer and quickened his pace, to walk away from his unpleasant companion. But Levake would not be shaken off, and as the two were passing a deserted restaurant he ordered the surgeon to halt. Arnold turned without shrinking. Levake had already drawn his pistol and his victim concluded he was to be killed then and there, but he resolved to tell the outlaw what he thought of him.

"I understand your game perfectly, Levake," he said after he had raked him terrifically. "Now, if you are going to shoot, do it. You haven't long to live yourself—make sure of that."

"No man can threaten me and live," retorted Levake harshly.

"I came up here, an unarmed man, on an errand of mercy."

"I didn't send for you."

"You would kill me just as quick if you had, Levake. What are you hesitating about? If you are going to shoot, shoot."

Throwing back his right arm, and fingering the trigger of his revolver as a panther lashes his tail before springing, Levake stepped back and to one side. As he did so, with the fearless surgeon still facing him, a man stepped from behind the screen door of the deserted restaurant. It was Bob Scott.

The old and deadly feud between the Indian and the outlaw brought them now, for the first time in months, face to face. In spite of his iron nerve Levake started. Scott, slightly stooped and wearing the familiar slouch hat and shabby coat in which he was always seen, regarded his enemy with a smile.

So sudden was his appearance that Levake could not for an instant control himself. If there was a man in the whole mountain country that Levake could be said to be afraid of, it was the mild-mannered, mild-spoken Indian scout. Where Scott had come from, how he had got through the pickets posted by Levake himself—these questions, for which he could find no answer, disquieted the murderer.

Arnold, reprieved from death as by a miracle, stood like a statue. Levake, with his hand on his pistol, had halted, petrified, at the sight of Scott.

The latter, eying the murderer with an expression that might have been mistaken for friendly, had not Levake known there could be no friendship among decent men for him, broke the silence: "Levake, I have a warrant for you."

The words seemed to shake the spell from the outlaw's nerves. He answered with his usual coolness: "You've waited a good while to serve it."

"I've been a little busy for a few days, Levake," returned Scott, with the same even tone. "I kind of lost track of you." But his words again disconcerted Levake. The few men who now watched the scene and knew what was coming stood breathless.

Levake, moistening his dry lips, spoke carefully: "I don't want any trouble with you here," he said. "When this town fight is over, bring your warrant around and I'll talk to you."

"No," returned Scott, undisturbed, "I might lose track of you again. You can come right along with me, Levake."

With incredible quickness the outlaw, half-turning to cover Scott, fired. The cat-like agility of the Indian answered the move in the instant it was made. Scott was, in fact, the first scout from whom mountain men learned to fire a revolver without aiming it and it was not without reason that Levake sought no encounter with him. For Scott to draw and fire was but one movement, and hating Levake as a monster, the Indian had long been ready to meet him as he met him now, when he should be forced to face him fairly.

A fusillade of shots rang down the street. The air between the two men, feinting like boxers in their deadly duel, filled with whitish smoke. Arnold, stunned by the suddenness of the encounter, jumped out of range. In the next moment he saw Levake sink to the sidewalk. Scott, springing upon him like a cat, knelt with one hand already on his throat; with the other he wrung a second revolver from Levake's hand. The surgeon ran to the two men.

Levake, panting, lay desperately wounded, as Scott slowly released his grip upon him. The Indian rose as the surgeon approached, but Levake, his eyes wide open, lay still.

"You are wounded, Bob," cried Arnold, tearing the stained sleeve of Scott's coat from his shoulder. The scout shook his head.

"We're in danger here," he replied, glancing hurriedly up the street. "We must get this fellow away."

The two picked the wounded man from the ground and started quickly down street with him. The shooting, now so frequent all over the town, had attracted little attention outside the few that had witnessed the swift duel, and the two railroad men made good progress with their burden before the alarm was spread. But the surgeon saw that the strain was telling on Scott, whose shoulder was bleeding freely. He had even ordered his companion to drop his burden and run, when he heard a shout and saw Bill Dancing running across from the barricade to their aid.

FOR SCOTT TO DRAW AND FIRE WAS BUT ONE MOVEMENT.

Half a dozen of the rioters, shouting threats and imprecations, were hastening down Front Street after Levake and his captors to rescue their prisoner. Scott, reloading his revolver as Dancing relieved him of his end of the burden, stood free to cover the retreat. He fired a warning shot at the nearest of their pursuers. A scattering pistol fire at long range followed. But the railroad men crossed the square in safety, and the big lineman, with Levake in his arms, carried him single-handed into the barricade.

The surgeon and Bob Scott followed close. Bucks was first to meet the wounded scout, and the railroad men, jubilant at Levake's capture, ran to Scott and bore him down with rough welcome. Levake was laid upon a bench in the station and Scott followed to his side. Arnold, joining the scout, made ready to dress the wound in his shoulder.

"See to Levake first, doctor," said Scott, "he needs it the most."

As he spoke, Dancing hurried into the room. "Bob, the car shops are on fire."

Scott ran to the east window. It was true. The rioters, supplied with oil and torches, had made their way in the darkness through Callahan's picket line near the river and set fire to the shops.

Stanley was eating a hasty supper in the despatchers' office.

Within a few minutes the blaze could be seen from all the east windows of the station. Almost at the same moment, through the north windows fire was seen breaking out in one of the big stores in Front Street. As Stanley rose from his midnight meal, Atkinson ran in with word that a band of rioters, well armed, had attacked a train of boarding-cars defended by the roundhouse men.

The sky, bright again with the flame of conflagration, made a huge dome of red, lighting the railroad yards across which men were now hurrying to make fresh dispositions for the emergency.

The vigilante leaders saw impending, in the Front Street fire, the ruin of their business property. There were no longer men enough left to fight the flames and guard the fire-fighters. A point had been reached in which life and property were no longer taken into account, and efforts to restore law and order were facing complete failure. It was then that the most radical of all measures, the last resort of organized society in its resolve to defend itself, was discussed. The vigilantes, as well as the railroad men, now realized that but one measure remained for saving Medicine Bend and that was the extermination of the outlaws themselves.

CHAPTER XXIV

The men in the barricade were lined up for orders. Ammunition was passed and volunteers were called to form a charging party. The vigilantes formed in the glare of the burning shops.

From the head-quarters of the rioters in Front Street came scattering shots and cries as a huge volume of sparks shot up into the black sky. Ten men under Hawk and ten under Dancing made the supporting party for the vigilantes, who asked only that a line of retreat be kept open. This Stanley had undertaken to provide. Atkinson, making a wide détour back of the station, led his men down the railroad tracks and, reaching a point where concealment was no longer possible, double-quicked up Fort Street and charged with his party across the little park.

They had already been seen. A line of men, posted behind the places that line Front Street at that point, opened fire. It was the worst possible answer to make to men in the temper of the scattered line that swept up the street in the glare of the burning buildings. Wounded men dropped out of the charge, but those that went on carried with them a more implacable determination. Re-forming their line under cover of the cedars at the corner of Fort Street, they directed an effective fire into the dance halls adjoining, and the rioters hiding within scurried from them like rats.

But the vigilantes were intent first of all on capturing and burning the hall known as the Three Horses, and the rioters rallied to its defence. As the place was assailed, the doors were barred and a sharp fire was poured through the windows. The assailants were driven back. Bill Dancing, heated and stubborn, refused to retreat and, picking up a sledge dropped by a fleeing vigilante, attacked the barred doors single-handed.

The street, swept by the bullets of the fray, rang with the splitting blows of the heavy hammer, as the lineman, his long hair flying from his forehead, swung at the thick panels. Within, the gamblers tried to shoot him from the windows, but he stood close and his friends kept up a constant supporting fire that drove the defenders back.

From above they hurled chairs and tables down on Dancing, but his head seemed furniture-proof, and scorning to waste time in dodging he hammered away, undaunted, until he splintered the panels and the stout lock-stiles gave. The vigilantes, running up, tore through the door chains with crowbars and rushed the building.

The fight in the big room lasted only a moment. The rioters crowded toward the rear and escaped as best they could. Vigilantes with torches made short work of the rest of it. Dancing stove in a cask of alcohol, and as the attacking party ran out of the front door a torch was flung back into the spreading pool.

A great burst of fire lighted the street. The next moment the long building was in flames.

Emboldened by this success and driving the outlaws from their further retreats, the vigilantes fired one after another of the gaudy places that lined the upper street. Met by close shooting at every turn, the rioters were driven up the hill and fighting desperately were pursued to cover by men now as savage as themselves. The scattered clashes were brief and deadly. The whole upper town was on fire. Men fleeing for their lives skulked in the shadows of the side streets and the constant scattering report of fire-arms added to the terrors of the night.

Hour after hour the conflagration raged and day broke at last on the smoking ruins of the town of Medicine Bend. The work of the vigilantes had been mercilessly thorough. Along the railroad track stiffened bodies hanging from the cross-bars of telegraph poles in the gloom of the breaking day told a ghastly story of justice summarily administered to the worst of the offenders. In the gloom of the smoking streets stragglers roamed unmolested among the ruins; for of the outlaws, killed or hunted out of the town, none were now left to oppose the free passage of any one from end to end of Medicine Bend.

CHAPTER XXV

The victory was dear, but none murmured at its cost. Medicine Bend for once had been purged of its parasites.

At the railroad head-quarters Stanley, before daylight, was directing the resumption of operations so interrupted by the three days of anarchism on the mountain division. New men were added every hour to the pay-roll, and the smaller tradesmen of the town, ruined by the riots, were given positions to keep them until the town could be rebuilt.

The pressure on the operating department increased twofold with the resumption of traffic. Winter was now upon the mountains, but construction could not be stopped for winter. The enormous prizes for extending the line through the Rockies to meet the rival railroad heading east from California, spurred the builders to every effort to lengthen their mileage, and something unheard of was attempted, namely, mountain railroad-building in midwinter.

Levake, the leader among the mountain outlaws, was nursed back to life by the surgeon he had so nearly murdered. But his respite was a brief one. When new officers of the law were elected in Medicine Bend, the murderer was tried for one of his many crimes and paid on the scaffold the penalty of his cold-blooded cruelty. Rebstock, the fox, and his companion Seagrue escaped the exterminating raid of the vigilantes but fought shy of Medicine Bend for long afterward.

A few days after the riots Stanley sent for Bucks, who was holding a key among the operators downstairs, to come to his office.

"How long have you been a telegraph operator, Bucks?" he asked.

Bucks laughed in some embarrassment. "Since I was about twelve years old, sir."

"Twelve years old!" echoed Stanley in amazement. "Where did you learn to telegraph at twelve?"

Bucks hesitated again. "I never learned, sir!"

"What do you mean?"

"I used to sit in the telegraph office of the road when my uncle was superintendent, and I got used to hearing the sound of the instruments. I just woke up one morning and found I could telegraph. I couldn't the night before. That's the only way I ever learned, sir."

Stanley regarded the boy with interest. "How old are you now?"

"Seventeen."

"Very well. When you went to bed last night you were not a train despatcher: this morning you are." Bucks started. "If any one ever asks you," continued Stanley dryly, "how you learned to be a train despatcher, tell them just that."

"I don't want you to think you are old enough to be a despatcher," continued Stanley, as Bucks stammered his thanks, "for you are not. And I don't want you to think I like to make you one. I don't. Neither for your sake nor mine. I don't like to impose the responsibilities of a man on a boy. But I can't help it. We haven't the men, and we can't get them—and we must all, men and boys, pull together and just do the best we can—do you understand?"

"I understand everything, Colonel Stanley."

"I need not say much about what is before you. You have been sending despatchers' orders for years yourself. You know how many lives are held every minute in the despatchers' hand. Don't overrate your responsibility and grow nervous over it; and don't ever underestimate it. As long as you keep yourself fit for your work, and do the best you can, you may sleep with a clear conscience. Report to Mr. Baxter. Remember you are working with green trainmen and don't expect too much of them."

When Bucks signed a transfer and took his train-sheet that night at twelve o'clock, his chief anxiety was to keep the material trains going to Casement and everything eastbound was laid out in an effort to send the ties and rails west. Bucks set himself to keep pace with the good work done by the despatcher in the evening trick and for two hours kept his sheet pretty clean.

A heavy train of rails which he had been helping all the way west after midnight was then at Castle Springs, and Bucks gave its crew an order to meet the eastbound passenger train at Point of Rocks. It was three o'clock when a message came from the operator at Point of Rocks, saying the rail train had passed westbound. Bucks seized a key and silencing the wires asked for the passenger train. Nothing had been seen of it. He called up Bitter Creek, the first telegraph point west of Point of Rocks with an order to hold the passenger train. But the train had already gone.

The new dispatcher sprang up from the table frantic. Then, racing again to the key, he made the operator at Castle Springs repeat the order and assure him it had been delivered. Of this there could be no question. The freight crew had ignored or forgotten it, and were now past Point of Rocks running head-on against the passenger train. If the heavens had fallen the situation would have seemed better to Bucks. A head-on collision on the first night of his promotion meant, he felt, his ruin. As he sat overwhelmed with despair, trying to collect his wits and to determine what to do, the door opened and Bob Scott appeared.

The scout, with his unfailing and kindly smile, advanced and held out his hand. "Just dropped in to extend my congratulations."

Bucks looked at him in horror, his face rigid and his eyes set. Scott paused and regarded his aspect with surprise. "Something has happened," he said, waiting for the despatcher to speak.

"Bob!" exclaimed the boy in desperation, "No. has run past her meeting order at Point of Rocks with No. . They will meet head-on and kill everybody. My God! what can I do?"

In the dim light of the shaded oil lamp, Bucks, looking at the scout, stood the picture of despair. Scott picked up the poker and began to stir the fire and asked only a few questions and said little. However, when Bucks told him he was going to wake Stanley, whose sleeping-room adjoined his office at the end of the hall, Scott counselled no.

"He could do nothing," said Scott reflecting. "Let us wait a while before we do anything like that," he added, coupling himself with the despatcher in the latter's overwhelming anxiety. "The first news of the collision will come from Bitter Creek. It will be time enough then to call Stanley. Give your orders for a wrecking crew, get a train ready, and get word to Doctor Arnold to go with it."

Bucks, steadying himself under the kindly common-sense of his older friend, followed each suggestion promptly. Scott, who ordinarily would himself have been running around on the job, made no move to leave the room, thinking he could be of more service in remaining with the unfortunate despatcher. The yard became a scene of instant activity. And although no organization to meet emergencies of this kind had been as yet effected on the new division, the men responded intelligently and promptly with the necessary arrangements.

Everyone summoned tried to get into the dispatchers' room to hear the story repeated. Scott took it upon himself to prevent this, and standing in the anteroom made all explanations himself. He rejoined Bucks after getting rid of the crowd, and the moment the relief train reported ready the despatcher sent it out, that help might reach the scene of disaster at the earliest possible moment. Bucks, calmed somewhat but suffering intensely, paced the floor or threw himself into his chair, while Scott picked up the despatcher's old copy of "The Last of the Mohicans," and smoking silently sat immovable, waiting with his customary stoicism for the call that should announce the dreaded wreck.

The moments loaded with anxiety went with leaden feet while the two men sat. It seemed as if the first hour never would pass. Then the long silence of the little receiver was broken by a call for the dispatcher. Bucks sprang to answer it.

Scott watched his face as he sent his "Ay, ay." Without understanding what the instruments clicked, he read the expressions that followed one after the other across Bucks's countenance, as he would have read a desert trail. He noted the perplexity on the despatcher's face when the latter tried to get the sender of the call.

"Some one is cutting in on the line," exclaimed Bucks, mystified, as the sounder clicked. "Bob, it is Bill Dancing."

A pause followed. "What can it mean, his sending a message to me? He is between Bitter Creek and Castle Springs. Wait a moment!"

The receiver clicked sharp and fast. Scarcely able to control his voice in his anxiety, Bucks turned to the now excited scout: "The trains met between Bitter Creek and Castle Springs. There was no collision!"

Almost collapsing with the passing of the strain, Bucks faltered in his taking. Asking Dancing again for the story, Bucks took it more coolly and repeated it to his eager listener, as it came.

"Dancing was out with two men on the line to-day, repairing between Bitter Creek and Castle Springs. He didn't get done and camped beside the track for the night, to finish in the morning."

"Go on," exclaimed Scott.

"They shot a jack-rabbit——"

"Hang the jack-rabbit," cried Scott. "What about the trains?"

"You can't hurry Bill Dancing, Bob," pleaded Bucks. "You know that. Faster, Bill, faster," he telegraphed urgently.

"You will get it faster," returned the distant lineman far out in the mountains under the stars, as he talked calmly with the despatcher, "if you will go slower."

Bucks strangled his impatience. Dancing resumed, and the despatcher again translated for Scott.

"They cooked the jack-rabbit for supper——"

Scott flung his book violently across the room. "It tasted good," continued Dancing exasperatingly. "But the night was awfully cold, so they built a big camp-fire near the curve. The freight engineer saw the fire and thought it was a locomotive head-light. Then he remembered he had run past his meeting point. He stopped his train to find out what the fire was. When he told Bill what had happened they grabbed up the burning logs, carried them down the track, and built a signal fire for No. . And it came along inside five minutes——"

"And there they are!" concluded Bucks, wiping the dampness from his forehead.

The receiver continued to click. "Bill thought I would be worried and he cut in on the line right away to tell me what had happened."

"Now give your orders to No. to back up to Castle Springs and let the rail train get by. Recall your relief train," added Scott. "And bring that freight engineer in here in the morning and let Stanley talk to him for just about five minutes." The key rattled for a moment. Scott, going to the farthest corner of the room, picked up "The Last of the Mohicans." "Bucks," he murmured insinuatingly, as he sat down to look into the book again, "I want to ask you now, once for all, whether this is a true story?"

"Bob, put that book where it belongs and stop talking about it."

Scott hitched one shoulder a bit and returned to the fire, but he was not silenced.

"That reminds me, Bucks," he resumed after a pause, "there is another friend of yours here at the door, waiting to congratulate you. Shall I let him in?"

"I don't want any congratulations, Bob."

"I'll promise he doesn't say a single word, Bucks." As he spoke, Scott opened the hall door and whistled into the darkness. For an instant there was no response. Then a small and vague object outlined itself in the gloom, but halted questioningly on the threshold. Wagging his abbreviated tail very gently and carrying his drooping ears very low, Scuffy at length walked slowly into the room. Bucks hailed him with delight, and Scuffy bounding forward crouched at his feet.

111

"I can't do a thing with him over at the ranch," complained Scott, eying the dog with a secret admiration. "He is eating the hounds up; doesn't give them a chance to pick a bone even after he's done with it."

"I'm afraid there is nothing to do with Scuffy, but to make a despatcher of him," returned Bucks, picking him up by the forepaws. "I can see very plainly it's going to be a dog's life most of the time."

CPSIA information can be obtained at www.ICGtesting.com
Printed in the USA
BVOW03s0027231014

372002BV00029B/296/P